Cosmic Latte

Rachel Trezise's semi-autobiographical novel *In and Out of the Goldfish Bowl* was published in 2000, to critical acclaim and a place on the Orange Futures List, is studied in Welsh Universities and at the University of Montreal. Her short story collection *Fresh Apples,* won the inaugural Dylan Thomas Prize in 2006. Trezise was writer in residence at the University of Texas in spring 2007. *Dial M for Merthyr* won the inaugural Max Boyce Prize in 2010. Her radio play *Lemon Meringue Pie* was broadcast on BBC Radio 4 in 2008. *Sixteen Shades of Crazy* was published by Blue Door in 2010. Her work has been translated into several languages and published all over the world.

Cosmic Latte

Rachel Trezise

Parthian, Cardigan SA43 1ED
www.parthianbooks.com
© 2013 Rachel Trezise
This edition published 2015
Cover design by Torben Schacht
This book has received a subsidy from SLOLIA Committee,
the Centre for Information on Literature in Bratislava, Slovakia.
ISBN 978-1-910409-03-9
Typeset by Elaine Sharples
Printed and bound by lightningsource.com
Published with the financial support of the Welsh Books Council
British Library Cataloguing in Publication Data
A cataloguing record for this book is available from the British
Library.

Contents

Czech Marionettes

The girl was leaning in a doorway off Václavské náměstí; one leg curled around the other, cheap summer dress showing too much swollen cleavage. The shoes were wrong; clumpy black mules studded with dulled rhinestones. But the ankles seemed familiar to Steffan: thin as parcel twine, the colour of strawberry milkshake. She sucked on her cigarette. Her eyes swept the street, this way and that. They came to rest on the pocket of Steffan's shorts where, of their own volition, his fingers had begun to smooth the leather binding of his wallet.

'You want to fuck?' she said, hard Slavic consonants. She threw her cigarette filter on the ground, crushing it with a twist of her graceless shoe, a move she might have learned watching Grease with Czech subtitles. Like many of the women in the city her eyelids were painted with a harsh stripe of sable black. He'd noticed it earlier, stood on the cool platform of the metro station, the metallic-green walls like giant blister packages of paracetamol, every three in four women passing by ticked with ebony eyeliner.

'The crown,' the girl said, gesturing at his pocket. 'You have it? You show me.'

Steffan took his wallet from his pocket, his wrist stiff and slow. His fingers were trembling, too clumsy to negotiate the clasp; he offered the wallet to her whole. She snatched it, tut-tutting. She unfurled some of the lavender-coloured notes, 5000 Kč, and threw the wallet back at his chest. 'For this anything you want,' she said, the foretaste of a smile on her mouth. Her front tooth was chipped at one edge. She spread the money like a hand of cards and fanned her face.

Steffan nodded, diffident.

'Two thousand up the ass if you like it,' she said. She stooped to stuff the cash into the toe of her shoe, her body jack-knifed, dry corkscrews of chestnut-coloured hair dangling at her waist. 'Come,' she said, beckoning him into a crowded tap-room where old men lined the bar. He followed her up a narrow stone staircase. The attic room was riddled with dry rot, a dim table lamp on the floor behind the door, a queen-sized bed the only piece of furniture. The wrought-iron frame was painted magenta pink, white slash marks cutting into the rails. She kicked her shoes off and sat on the bed, her legs curled around her. 'You want to know my name?' she asked.

Steffan shook his head. He sat down gingerly, next to her on the bed.

'You want to give me a name?'

He thought about it. 'Kuh-' he said dumbly, like a child stuck on phonics. He could see the name in his mind's eye, the curly tail of the y reeling, but the letters wouldn't pour down into his throat. The prostitute raised an eyebrow, waiting.

'No.' It was an insult to her memory. He feigned a cough. 'It's OK.'

The girl lifted herself up and straightened a leg, displaying it. Steffan's gaze focused on the nub of the fibula, so lumpy and distinct beneath the tightly clung skin. He bowed across the mattress, kissing the cold ankle bone over and over again.

Thirty minutes earlier he'd been at Rocky O'Reilly's with the rest of the stag party, the six of them hunched over a table in the backroom, downing Guinness and fry-ups for lunch. Philip had had T-shirts printed; mustard-yellow text on blue cotton, *Taffia on Tour*.

'Yesterday's got me horny for September,' said Jimmy, his mouth full of sausage meat. 'Fuck, I haven't handled a sharpshooter since Brecon last spring.' Jimmy Jizz was a TA. He came home from tours of duty with photographs of himself, topless and sunburned, a sniper propped on his hip. He handed out packs of US military-issue playing cards as if they were sticks of rock: Saddam Hussein the ace of spades. 'Four weeks and three days. I'm actually counting.' Dale was two weeks clear of a six-month tour of Helmand province, second battalion, Royal Welsh. 'What would you know about it, Jizz?' he asked Jimmy. 'Playing soldiers in the barracks?' He rolled his eyes and fashioned his fingers into hand guns. 'Peow, peow. You're not safe with a water pistol, mate.'

'I'll be back now,' Glyn, the bridegroom, said. The legs of his chair scraped against the floorboards as he stood and headed for the gents, skin drained of colour. He'd been up until 5 a.m that morning, drinking in the communal lounge with Philip, his first pint of the day going down like needles.

'Listen boys,' Philip said, voice conspiratorial as he watched Glyn retreat. 'I've got an idea for the best man speech. We'll get a big pile of door keys, right? And hand them out to the women before the wedding. When it comes to the dinner and my speech, I'll say this: "We all know that Glyn's had a highly illustrious career as a womaniser,"' his voice affecting an officious tone, like an onion rolling around the bottom of a tin bucket. '"But today it comes to an end. Today, Glyn has married his fiancée. This isn't going to be easy, ladies. But Glyn is taken now. Form an orderly queue at the table to return his house keys. We'll call it an amnesty, no questions asked. You know it's the right thing to do."' He turned his palms up, chuckling at his own ingenuity. 'Can you imagine?' he said. 'This long line of birds queuing up at the wedding table? We'll get dirty Delyth up as well!'

It was too much for Steffan. Talk of weddings, wives, women. He should have expected it, a stag weekend after all. But he thought he was getting better. At first, when somebody said 'my missus', 'my missus this', or 'my kid that', it had felt like a penknife twisting between his ribs. 'I'm going for a fag,' he said. He'd quit smoking five years earlier, in case it was reducing his sperm count. Nobody seemed to remember. Nobody followed him outside. He wandered aimlessly around the boulevard,

4

scanning the Art Nouveau architecture, reading plaques commemorating the Velvet Revolution. After a while he stumbled into a toy market on the edge of a side street. Tens of stalls cluttered with jigsaw puzzles, marzipan cakes, Russian dolls.

A stallholder called out to him, 'Hey you.' It was one of those American-English accents that Europeans picked up watching MTV. 'Genuine hand-carved marionettes. Neat gifts for the kids.' On the rail behind him hundreds of intricate lime-wood puppets hung from near-invisible strings: warty-faced witches, Santa Claus figures; pious Jews with ringlets and little felt hats, the sun reflecting in their miniature eyeglasses. The stallholder held up the puppet in his hand, a doll in a navy dress, yellow wool for hair, red bindis for cheeks. He worked its wires so that it walked on thin air, waving fanatically at Steffan. 'Go on,' the stallholder said. He handed the puppet to him. 'Try it out.'

Steffan took it, holding it by its smooth wooden handle. In sudden fear of one-upmanship he began tipping it from left to right, trying to make it dance. It only veered to one side, half paralysed. The stallholder clicked his tongue. 'Real Czech marionettes have no central rod. They're harder to work than the Sicilian or Burmese types,' he said, nonchalant, as though Steffan would know such things existed. Steffan shook his head, the cotton of his T-shirt cleaving against his skin. He tried again with the puppet and got its elbow jiggling sadly. He felt his temper rising. His brain seemed to balloon and press against the back of his skull. His hands scrabbled, pulling at the wires tangled around his broad knuckles. 'Huh,' he said, flinging the puppet onto the table in front of the stallholder. 'I haven't got any kids!' He plodded away from the market, berating himself for getting involved, the knot of frustration left half-tied and fist-like in his chest. That temper, hot and fast as pepper spray. He had no idea what would set it off next.

The prostitute unbuckled his belt. She pulled back her hair. 'How is that?' she said. 'You like it fast? Or slowly?' Through a tiny window above the skirting he could see a blast of spiky graffiti on the wall of the opposite building, the same spray-paint protests he'd seen all over Prague, all over Europe; foreign and futile. It was late in the afternoon, the sun bloodying the sky. He closed his eyes and he was back in Lombardy, two Julys ago, lying on the bank of a mercury-lined lake. It was his honeymoon. He held threads of his wife's hair, watching them turn bronze in his fingers. Afterwards they'd order dinner at the humble osteria they'd found and claimed. Stracotto d'asino served on chequered tablecloths; he didn't have the heart to tell her it was donkey-meat stew, but that's what it was. Donkey and horsemeat was the local speciality. They'd walk the food off on the Piazza Sordello, roaming the Corinthian pilasters in the basilica with its relic of holy blood. His wife was raised Catholic, but she didn't believe in Jesus. 'Jesus can kiss my arse,' she said once, watching news footage of children starving in Africa. Still, he couldn't keep her away from the candle stands and collection boxes. He'd wondered without any real conviction if that was the reason for her death. Had she been punished for her hypocrisy?

The last thing she ever did was buy two tins of odourless emulsion: strawberry cheesecake and soft lime. The insurance company filched them out of the boot of her crozzled Suzuki jeep and sent them to him via courier a week later. There was a table lamp too, crushed on impact, a rotating shade that sent Mickey-Mouse-shaped silhouettes sliding up the walls. He refused to believe what the police officers told him over a cup of too-sweet tea. From the dining table where he sat he could see a glass on the draining board stained with the imprint of her lip gloss, still half full with juice. When they left he took the flat-pack cot out of its box and erected it in less than ten minutes. She'd been nagging him about it for a month. Much later he drank the warm, gluey orange juice left on the draining board. He let go of a belch that threatened to turn to a string of vomit, and with it came a hazy realisation that she was in fact dead, the baby too. He was a widower.

Now he felt his stomach tighten.

'You are ready,' the prostitute said. She took off her bra and knickers, a matching set, black with turquoise flowers embroidered at the edges. They looked inappropriate, like a parsley garnish on a bag of chips. Naked she looked raw, pork-like. She wet two fingers and slipped them inside her. She crawled over him on the bed. Clawing at his T-shirt she saw the vast bruise on his ribcage, swirling and swollen, yellow in the middle, plum at the verge, like something from the solar system, an ultrasound. 'What is this?' she said pressing on it.

He opened one eye, frowning. 'From paintballing,' he said. 'Yesterday.'

She nodded without understanding, tugging his T-shirt down, patting its hem.

He'd had to join the foreign team to balance the numbers. They were a group of four German fashion models on a team-building exercise, twenty-year-olds with limbs like willow branches. Communication was problematic and on the Welsh side, John, Glyn, Philip, Dale and Jizz; two squaddies and a TA. He didn't have a chance. He thought he was alone, reloading cartridges under a larch tree on the outskirts of the arena when he heard a bough crack above him.

'Hasta la vista, Kraut lover.' Jizz was stretched along the length of a lower branch. He shot Steffan in the chest, then twice in the head as he curled up to protect himself. Steffan had spent the evening snatching the tiny bottles of shampoo from the other boys' en-suites, scrubbing the tenacious blue paint out of his hair with the hard Czech water. The others watched pornography in the communal lounge, schoolboy whooping and chuckling over the money shots.

The prostitute went at it, something of a gymnast about her, her legs flexed to isosceles triangles, the creak of the mattress a flawless samba rhythm. Steffan squeezed his eyelids together, concentrating, trying to get back to Lombardy. Instead there was another memory of a quickie in the utility room. She'd been folding clean washing, the smell of the powder in the air, fresh and simultaneously caustic. 'Kuh,' he sighed, his head raised in wonder. It was only a few minutes in. He took deep breaths, trying to steady himself. And then again: 'Kuh.'

The girl stopped kindly, pausing until his breathing returned to normal.

Something else. 'Think of something else,' he thought. The wedding night came back to him, the lace bodice and ball gown skirt, half an hour of drunken fumbling at the tens of eyelets and grommets, only to find out that she'd had her period: a patch of dried brown blood on ivory silk. 'I knew that would happen,' she said. 'I've been worrying about that since I started my periods when I was twelve. That's how unlucky I am; a period on my wedding night. I could curdle milk just by walking into a room.' She'd brought it on herself, worrying. No sex, then. They lay in the middle of their bed, him spooning her; their skin turned mottled from the heat.

They consummated it three days later. She was trying bikinis on for the honeymoon in their bedroom, wearing a red and white two-piece when he'd walked in to change after work.

It was happening now. He couldn't stop it. He wrenched at the girls wrists. 'Kuh-Kathy,' he mewed, his voice feminine. The girl hoisted herself up and around, glancing at him over her shoulder. 'You are done,' she said, as if he was a slab of brisket she'd dragged from the oven. She bowed to retrieve her underwear, her sex turned to an abrupt, vermillion wound. She produced a waste bin from under the bed, the kind he'd seen in hospitals for sharps – bright yellow plastic. 'For condom,' she said. She turned her back to him, running a lipstick along the straight line of her mouth.

'Would you sit with me for a few minutes?' he asked, mindful of how clichéd and pathetic it sounded. But the clichés were always true. It wasn't the sex he missed particularly. It was the company and the head scratches. Kathy had a way of scratching him, with the flat of her fingernail pushed hard against his scalp. He couldn't buy it from a masseuse. He couldn't replicate it with his own hand, made numb by his own weight, the way teenagers tried to masturbate. He patted the bed, feigning confidence. 'Something, please?' he said. The anaesthetic in the orgasm had faded too quickly. He was desperate again.

The prostitute studied him, considering it. 'Not here,' she said. 'Downstairs. You can buy me a drink.' He followed her down the cramped staircase, through the tap-room, and out onto the street, her mules knocking on the pavement. 'You are new to this,' she said; a statement, not a question. Steffan continued walking, unaware of his destination. He saw the insignia of the nightclub Glyn had chosen, a row of pearls, a sticker in the window of a pavement-side ticket kiosk. Finally the prostitute turned into a bar; Americana deco, duck-egg blue furniture, a Wurlitzer jukebox with real 45s resting against the back wall. She ordered two whiskeys.

'Would you eat donkey?' he asked her as the tender poured the drinks.

'Don. Key?' she said, as if the syllables were two separate words. Already he knew that she would. There was nothing finical about this one. She wouldn't worry about what Jesus thought. She wouldn't hesitate too long at a junction. She'd inhale paint fumes for fun. She lifted her drink and made a toast, said, 'Here's to the best you ever had.'

He laughed at her sass as she downed her drink. 'I have to work now,' she said. She put her glass on the bar and turned out of the pub. Steffan watched her disappear. She wasn't the best he'd ever had, not even close.

The girl gone, he was shocked that he was still there, slumped on the barstool, as real as the parquet floor underneath him. It was the same after Kathy died. After the orange juice and the realisation, he'd expected to perish, to simply stop being, to shrink, to rot from the inside out. But he just kept on going. The clock kept on ticking, minute after slow, empty minute. Sometimes when he woke in the morning there was that thing the doctor warned him about, the idea that it had been a nightmare, and then the awful truth. It wasn't a nightmare: the reality was worse than anything his subconscious was capable of. But mostly he was amazed to find that he was still alive, that there was more time, oodles and oodles of time, just waiting to be filled. Time was infinite without people to share it with. And now another realisation: you had to accept when your time with a person was up. You could conjure memories, but you couldn't conjure people. You can't put your arms around a memory. He finished his whiskey.

Back on Štěpánská the stags were still hunched at their table in the Irish bar, watching ice hockey on a projected screen in the corner, singing Cardiff City football club songs. 'When the coal comes from the Rhondda on the Taff Vale railway line, with my little pick and shovel-' Philip broke off, gazing glass-eyed at Steffan. 'Here he is. Where've you been? We've been waiting here in case you got lost. You've wasted an hour's valuable drinking time.'

Steffan shrugged. He put the advance tickets for the nightclub down on the table, laminated cards, a looping row of pearls in the top right corner. 'Couldn't let Glyn spend his last weekend of freedom in an Irish bar, could I? Welsh we are.' He wrinkled his nose. 'Not my kind of thing, dance music and lap dancers. Not my stag party though is it?'

'That's my job,' Philip said.

'No, your job's the next round.' Steffan noticed the puppet on the table, half the size of the ones from the market: a Long John Silver character with a peg leg and crooked teeth. Dale saw the confusion on Steffan's face. 'Guy came around selling them,' he said, voice low with remorse. 'Bought one for the boy, you know.' He whipped it from the surface of the table, throwing it onto a shelf underneath, out of sight.

'It's OK, Dale,' Steffan said, going for his wallet. 'I'll pay for it. I'm his godfather.'

Dale peered at Steffan, uncertain.

Steffan nodded. 'It's OK,' he said. 'You've got a kid. You've got a wife. It's OK.'

The Prayer for Eggs

It was after six when the airless corridor spat Levi into the concourse at the centre of Ben Gurion airport. Immediately he saw his name, **Gruenembaum**, scrawled in black Sharpie on a piece of brown cardboard. The man holding the placard was old and bespectacled; as Levi approached him he realised that it was the Rabbi, his greyed side-curls tucked behind his fleshy ears. Levi patted himself down, checking that his prayer shawl was in place, the strings hanging prominent. 'Rabbi?' he murmured, tentative. There was always the chronic sense of guilt.

Rabbi Friedman slapped the teenager's back. 'What? You think I'd send a driver? Welcome to the Holy Land.' He threw the placard aside and took the handle of Levi's suitcase, dragging it haphazardly through the bustle, Levi struggling to keep up. 'You see this? By Salvador Dalí?' The Rabbi gestured at a big brass menorah on the pavement outside the terminal. 'Yes?' Levi stopped to scrutinise the sculpture, but the Rabbi only carried on ahead, the wheels of the suitcase scraping on the concrete. From the corner of his eye Levi saw a female IDF soldier stood at the entrance to the parking lot, her bronze skin glistening under a street lamp, her bicep rippling as she shifted her Uzi to her opposite shoulder, onyx-black spiral curls down to her tuchus. It was November and the sun was setting, but the air was too hot to breathe. 'The Holy Land?' he thought to himself. 'This place is hotter than hell.'

'Here,' the Rabbi pointed at a tiny green hatchback parked in the front row.

After fifteen minutes they found themselves in a traffic standstill on Rehov Dizengoff, a boulevard as wide as any Manhattan avenue. Groups of mixed-sex youths congregated in front of café bars, dressed immodestly in knee-length skirts and short-sleeved blouses, the points of their cigarettes like miniature orange flares demanding Levi's attention. In the part of Brooklyn where he lived the women covered their elbows and legs, and if for some reason they didn't, the men around them were obliged to look the other way. He spied a tattoo and body piercing studio. What kind of Jew got a tattoo? he thought, the admonishment from Leviticus ringing in his ears. 'You shall not make gashes in your flesh for the dead, or incise any marks on yourself: I am the Lord.' And then he realised what the electronic vending machines peppering the roadside were dispensing: pornographic DVDs. More naked flesh on display than in the window at the glatt kosher butchers. 'How far to the yeshiva?' he asked the Rabbi, stifling a splutter, remembering his afternoons in Prospect Park, and the pornography he'd found there.

'Ach, not far,' Friedman replied, his eyes glued to the road. 'We're near Jaffa. You know the oranges?' He pointed out a second sculpture, a brightly coloured wheel with the notched teeth of a fan belt. 'Designed by Yaacov Agam. You know it used to spurt water? It's broken now.'

'And how far to Jerusalem?' Levi asked.

'Jerusalem?' Friedman said, as if he'd been accused of something. 'Jerusalem. Why? Our yeshiva here is as holy as the Candle of Israel, as holy as anything they have there. We pride ourselves on bringing troubled young men back to Hashem and we can do that perfectly well here in Tel Aviv. Jerusalem is Jerusalem, of course.' He sighed. 'But!' He wagged his finger at Levi. 'You'll see we won't be outdone, thank you very much.'

'I need to go to the Wall,' Levi said. Surely Friedman knew the Wailing Wall was the holiest place in all of Judaism save for the Temple Mount itself. 'I have a note,' he said. 'A prayer. You see my grandmother is ill, Rabbi Friedman. Alzheimer's.'

'Terrible!' Friedman said.

'My mother's written a note pleading for her health. She wants me to put it in the wall the way they do. You know?' He smoothed his hand over his breast pocket going for the handwritten note. And then he remembered what he'd done eight hours earlier, bored witless in the JFK departures lounge; he'd written his own little prayer on the other side of the note: 'Sex please God. Just one time. Real sex.' He dropped his hand to his lap, jammed his fingers between his thighs, and snapped his legs shut on his fingers. 'Sure,' the Rabbi said, a new compassion to his tone. 'You'll get a day to yourself after Sabbath. You'll go then, two hours by bus.' Levi nodded, relieved. 'Have you prayed with tefillin today?' the Rabbi asked, an afterthought.

'Yes sir,' Levi said.

The car pulled off the road, onto a driveway leading to a modest stone building, palm trees lining the boundaries. Levi had never seen a palm tree before. 'Here we are,' the Rabbi said. A second Rabbi appeared at the entrance, clapping his hands and running towards the car. 'Another student,' he sang gleefully. 'Another student to study the word of Hashem? Blessed is God!' The Rabbis took the suitcase from the trunk, top and tail. It was properly dark now and Levi's sense of hearing increased to compensate for the lack of light. He was sure he heard a female giggle, a sweet ha-ha-hee in the distance. He squinted past the trees, searching for the owner of the laugh, but the wheels of the suitcase on the gravel spoiled his concentration. 'What are you waiting for?' Friedman called back to him. 'Come, come, welcome to Aviv Zion Yeshiva young Mr. Gruenembaum.' It was not the kind of establishment Levi's mother would have expected. In the hall, a bookcase half-filled with English language novels: *Harry Potter and the Philosopher's Stone*, *The Da Vinci Code*, *Black Beauty*. They'd be considered illicit in Brooklyn. Friedman caught Levi, head lopsided, staring at the spines. 'Ah,' he said, unsurprised. 'How can we recognise ourselves if we don't look outside?'

'Indeed!' Levi said. His point exactly! Ultra-orthodox Judaism was stuck in a rut, conversing only with itself, like some crazed bum on the streets of the Lower East Side. 'Charity,' Friedman said, 'from the bookshop on Allenby. We don't look a gift horse in the mouth here, but we'd prefer our students to read Hebrew.' He showed the new arrival to the eight-bed dormitory, heaving his case onto an empty cot pushed up against the furthest wall. A boy sat on the next bed along, a naked picture of Kate Moss in his lap, a half-page torn from a fashion magazine, one of his skinny red side-curls sucked into his mouth. 'This is Aaron from Anaheim,' the Rabbi said, gesturing at the teenager. 'And this is Levi, from Borough Park. Remember you only get one chance to make a first impression. Be nice to each other. Dinner downstairs in half an hour.' The Rabbi disappeared out of the door. Aaron glanced once at Levi and held the photograph up for him to see. 'You notice it yet?' He pointed at the model's breasts. 'Girl's got an inverted left nip.'

Photographs of naked women are what Levi had come to Israel to avoid and after only forty minutes in the country he'd encountered them, twice. All he needed now was for Aaron from Anaheim to produce a pack of pink and white marshmallows from under his pillow and the culmination of sin that had brought him here would be replete and in its correct order. If Levi had to calculate the exact moment, the point where he fell off the rails, he'd choose a balmy June afternoon; the instant he realised his new Hebrew teacher, Rabbi Bolinger, was virtually blind. Levi was answering a question about

17

Judeo-Arabic when he dropped his pencil on the floor. He kneeled to retrieve it but the boy at the next desk along accidentally kicked it out into the aisle. Levi crawled after it. The whole escapade took around eight seconds but had seemed like minutes on end. When finally Levi had his pencil in his fist he stood triumphantly in the aisle. 'Correct, Mr. Gruenembaum,' Rabbi Bolinger was saying, talking in earnest to the thin air above Levi's empty chair. Levi took advantage of the man's disability at the next available opportunity, getting his study partner to cover for him. It wasn't an aversion to Hebrew per se. He liked Rabbi Bolinger. He only wanted to get one over on the yeshiva, on authority in general. He'd spent his snatched period of free time, sitting on a bench in nearby Prospect Park, spying on a secular couple a few benches along. They were eating hotdogs and kissing intermittently, unable to get through a meal without touching one another. Even from a distance he could see they were happy. His gaze fell to the garbage can on his right, and the corner of a magazine curled out over its lip. Magazines were anathema in his culture, but so were hotdogs, secular couples, kissing, touching and happiness: the whole Megillah. His entire life revolved around the Torah and the Talmud, study and prayer. He scooted closer to the can. There was a stack of magazines: pornographic. He flicked one open to a picture of a blonde lady lying on her back, her legs spread wide. The expression on the woman's face was pained, but somehow he knew she wasn't in pain. The image did something to him, deep in his belly, a part of himself he'd never felt before. He gasped: an age old gust of air that seemed to have been trapped in his lungs since birth, his heartbeat, a hammer on cloth.

When he got back to the park two days later, the magazines were gone. He checked the next can along, and the one after that. He rifled through the garbage like a bag lady who hadn't eaten for a week. In the sixth garbage can he found one lone magazine, its cover stained with soda. It was a *Hustler*, the women smooth-skinned and big-busted, their triangular tufts of hair blonde and neat. Taking no chances he stuffed it into his prayer bag and carried it home. That night his mother caught him masturbating, the *Hustler* opened to its centrefold and set down on the bed next to his skeletal chest. She was carrying a pile of laundry, which she dropped, a look of real pain in her face, her eyes shrunk. 'Vilda Chaya,' she chanted as she ran from the spectacle. 'Wild animal.' Nothing is more despicable in Judaism than a man who wastes his seed. And yet it wasn't the final straw. Life continued as normal for a fortnight, the incident unmentioned. Then, returning from yeshiva on an idle Tuesday evening, Levi was confronted by his father, an empty marshmallow bag in his hand. 'Marshmallows?' Mr. Gruenembaum said. He clipped Levi around the ear, a clump of the teenager's side-curl catching in his wedding ring and ripping right out of his scalp. 'You are frei now?' Levi tried to blame the plastic wrapper on his sixteen-year-old sister Deena, or one of his younger siblings; something picked from the street for use as a plaything. His father shook his head, resolute. 'Under your pillow, Levi. Your pillow. Marshmallows! The flesh of pigs. What next?

Cheeseburgers? I'll kill you myself first. Death or reform school?' His father bawled, tiny baubles of spittle landing on Levi's face. 'Death or Israel, son? It's your choice.'

Dinner that evening was shakshouka, in honour of Levi, the new arrival, prepared by Rabbi Friedman's own hands. The students sat around the dining table in their waistcoats and yarmulkes, Rabbi Silverman leading the prayer for eggs. 'Blessed are You, Lord our God, King of the Universe, by whose word all things came to be.'

'A delicacy here in Israel,' Friedman said, watching Levi take his first mouthful of the sloppy red mixture. 'And a change from all that gefilte fish.' When they'd finished eating he announced two hours' free time, excusing the six boys not listed on the clean-up rota. 'You smoke?' Aaron asked. Levi shook his head. 'Too bad,' said Aaron, heading for the front door. Levi followed him anyway, not knowing what else to do. 'They don't lock the doors?' he asked, incredulous.

'Lock the doors? What d'you think it is, kid? Borstal? News flash, man. You lucked out. This place couldn't afford to keep us in line, even if it wanted to. Cheapest reform school in all of Israel.' He stood under the porch roof, lighting his cigarette. 'Hey, let me tell you a joke,' he said as he blew out a virgin plume of grey fug. 'There's this shiksa, right, a fine-looking shiksa, and she's got a real thing about guys like us.' He smiled at Levi. 'It's the ringlets, dude, something about them just turns her wet-' He stopped talking suddenly, squinting into the darkness. 'Tzippy?' he called out, his hand curled around his mouth. 'Tzippy, that you, you crazy lady?'

A woman emerged, hologram-like, a pale turquoise slip clinging to her hip bones, her perfectly round face framed with a shock of black tangled hair. She was thirty years old, maybe more. 'Not so fine,' Aaron said under his breath. He looked from Levi to the woman and back again. 'Oh, you two haven't met,' he said. 'This is Tzippy; lovely girl, lives at the institution up there on the hill.' Levi swallowed hard. They were not supposed to be left alone with members of the opposite sex. 'She won't bite,' Aaron said. 'Not unless you want her to.' He turned to Tzippy, speaking slowly. 'This is Levi, Tzip, the new boy. Why don't you take him for a walk? Show him around the grounds, huh? He ain't seen them yet.' The woman stood still, patient, waiting. Aaron nudged Levi down the first step. 'Go on,' he said. 'Enjoy.'

The woman walked westward towards a scrub bush three yards away from the house, her head hung low. The moon highlighted her calf muscles and turned her white skin Alice-blue. She was barefoot, her toes spread as she circumnavigated the scrub, inching her way down a grassy incline. 'So, you know this place well?' Levi asked her, following hesitantly, peeking back now and then at Aaron, who'd turned to face the front door. She waved at him feverishly, instructing him to follow her down the slope. He took a few steps, slowly growing confident. He could see the horseshoe curve of the coast, and the Tel Aviv skyline beyond. He hit a patch of moss and slipped, landing on his butt. Before he could get up the woman was on top of him, fingernails scratching at his flies. He reached up to push her off but didn't connect. He dropped his arms at his sides, paralysed with anticipation. She'd got past his pants and into his underwear. 'Are you sure?' he whispered, voice high as giraffes. The woman held him, squeezed in her hand, her bug eyes regarding him remotely. For one awful eternity, he thought she was going to stop. Instead she guided him into her and she sat on him, wriggling. It lasted two minutes, maybe three. She was gone before Levi could raise his head off the ground.

Aaron was still on the porch, dousing his cigarette in a sand bucket. 'You did it?' he said as he straightened up. 'Mazel Tov.' He elbowed Levi in the ribs.

'She did it,' Levi protested, the blood drained from his legs. 'If I'd said no it would have been rape.' He was exultant but exhausted. He could have slept right there, standing up. 'Yeah, she's friendly,' Aaron said. 'She likes to make the newbies feel welcome.'

After Sabbath Levi took the bus to Jerusalem, his mother's note folded in his shirt pocket. 'You'll arrive at Jaffa Road,' Friedman said, dropping him off at the bus station. 'Take a cab to the old city. Be sure to take an Israeli cab, not an Arab cab. Yellow licence plates. Remember! Yellow licence plates, not blue.' Levi took a window seat on the bus, flanked by an IDF soldier. Ten minutes into the journey the soldier was asleep, his head on Levi's shoulder, his Uzi in his lap. Levi took the note from his pocket and read his handwriting over, the sun beaming on the right side of his face. 'Sex please God. Just one time. Real sex.' So maybe there was a God, he thought, and maybe He did provide. He considered adding 'more' between the 'Just' and the 'one', but knew that that was selfish. He should have been concentrating on his grandmother's ill health, and besides, going for the pen in his prayer bag would disturb the sleeping soldier and maybe he'd wake up in a daze, thinking he was under attack, reach for his gun and shoot the whole bus up. Levi'd got what he'd asked for. He'd rewrite his mother's note when he got to the Wailing Wall, in capitals so that God had more chance of seeing it amongst all those hundreds of other prayers. He watched the landscape from the window, knowing that he was close to Jerusalem when the vast highway subsided, the jagged black hills growing steeper, freckled with dry green scrub.

The bus station was chaos. Soldiers everywhere, taking up posts and positions, fingers curled over triggers; an abysmal, resonant shrieking sound from outside. Levi didn't know if this was how it always was, or if something had happened. A man in a Hawaiian shirt was leaning against a pillar, watching the commotion nonplussed. 'What's going on?' Levi asked him.

'Suicide bomber,' the man said, eyes flitting around. 'It happens from time to time,' a mocking tone to his voice. Levi made his way to the bus station exit. A camera crew were reporting from the pavement, interviewing a survivor. There was a black hat hovering at the perimeter of the crowd, an eighteen-year-old, skinny, like Levi. 'Shalom,' Levi said, approaching him.

'Nine dead,' the boy replied in Yiddish, semi-acknowledging Levi. 'And this woman, shrapnel buried in the hardcover book she was reading. She survived the exact same way forty years ago when her street blew up. She always reads hardcovers.'

'So which way to the taxi stand?' Levi asked him.

'This is the taxi stand,' the boy said. Together they scanned the road, searching for taxis. There were only soldiers, army cavalcades, ambulances. 'I have to get to the wall,' Levi told him. 'My grandmother has Alzheimer's,' he added uselessly. The black-hat boy sucked his teeth. 'The old city's blockaded. It will be for hours. That's the way it happens. They have to secure the streets, get the phones on. Come back tonight.'

Levi shook his head. 'I have to get back to Tel Aviv; last bus at six.' The boy searched Levi's eyes, confused. 'Tel Aviv? The city of sin. Why not Jerusalem? Why not the Candle of Israel? Are you a real pious Jew?' Levi didn't see the wall that day, only a photograph of it; a postcard in the gift shop in the bus station: three IDF soldiers leant against it in prayer; their Uzis hung on their shoulders. Levi smoothed his fingertips over the gigantic yellow stones, the card glossy against his skin. He said his own prayer for his grandmother, his eyes screwed closed. 'God, if you can send a woman from the institute to pop my sex cherry, you can cure Bubbe. You have to or I'm going to die of guilt.' When he opened his eyes the proprietor was standing in front of him, a sweeping brush in his hand. 'You buying that card or not?'

Levi shook his head.

'You touch the cards you have to buy them. What do you think this is? An art gallery? You buy or you leave.' He brushed at the toes of Levi's shoes, sweeping him out of the shop. 'Get, get, go on.' When Levi got back to the Yeshiva in Tel Aviv, Aaron was stood on the porch, smoking. 'What up, dude?' he said.

'Suicide bomb in the street outside the bus station,' said Levi. 'Couldn't put my note in the wall. Couldn't get to the Old City.' He opened the front door, stepping inside. His conscience wouldn't survive another roll in the grass with Tzippy, the moon-faced nymphomaniac. 'Wait,' Aaron said. 'You went all the way to Jerusalem to put a note in the wall? You know there's a company who'll do that for you? You can fax it, man. It'll take, like, two minutes. There's a fax machine in Friedman's office. He ain't here. Popped out to the market for groceries.'

'You can fax a note to the Wailing Wall?'

'Uh-huh. Guy walks down there once a day with the messages; stuffs them right into the gaps.' Levi climbed the stairs to the second floor, and Rabbi Friedman's office, his hand on his shirt pocket. He knocked twice on the door, checking that Silverman wasn't inside; after a few moments of silence he turned the handle. Friedman's desk overlooked the view to the west: the harbour and the outcrop of rock where it's said Andromeda was rescued by Perseus. Had the Rabbi been there four nights earlier when Tzippy got her way with Levi, he would have got an eyeful of that too. Levi took the Israeli business directory from the bookcase, searching under K for Kotel, the Hebrew name for the wall. He found a company called Wailing Wall Couriers, 'Prayers and messages carefully hand delivered'. He called the number listed and the employee on the other end of the line took a payment of eleven shekels off Levi's emergency credit card. 'So I just send it?' Levi asked.

'As soon as you like. Email or fax.' Email was out of the question, the internet forbidden. 'I'll fax it,' Levi said, 'right now; I'm going to fax it.' He put the phone down and reached into his pocket, unfolding the note, the paper soft and worn. He wanted to write a brand new one but there were footsteps on the landing outside, students running past. He didn't have much time. He turned the machine on, dialling the number, feeding the original prayer into its slit of a mouth. The transmission started. It sounded like something chewing on bone. In fact the noise was so loud Levi didn't notice Rabbi Silverman coming in. 'Mr. Gruenembaum? Is everything alright? You know the Rabbi's office is out of bounds?' He was standing behind Levi, his hand pressed on the back of the chair.

Levi swung around, throwing him off. 'Oh, Rabbi Silverman-' his lips flapping open and closed, searching for words. 'I'm sorry. I'm just borrowing the fax machine. He said I could, if it was urgent.' A copy of the facsimile he was sending to the Wailing Wall Couriers coughed out onto the paper tray. Levi recognised his handwriting, the first words. 'Sex please God...' He grabbed at the paper, hiding it from Silverman, practically ripping it out of the bowels of the ancient machine.

'So it's urgent?' Silverman asked.

'And private,' Levi said. He folded the paper, stuffing it into his shirt pocket. He tried a little small talk. 'Nice weather today?' he said.

'It's Israel, Mr. Gruenembaum. The weather is almost always nice here.' Silverman went for the machine, lifting a flap-like contraption, looking underneath. There was the worn page, the original prayer, Levi's mother's spidery handwriting. Levi seized it, scrunching it into the ball of his hand. He walked backwards out of the office, as if from the Wailing Wall itself. 'If I catch you in here again there'll be repercussions,' the Rabbi said. Levi smiled, his teeth gritted. 'Of course, Rabbi Silverman. No more urgencies.' He closed the office door behind him, kicking the balustrade. Shit with shakshouka! Eleven shekels! All for the wrong prayer.

A few days later Levi called home. 'Hello,' his sister Deena answered. 'I'll get Mameh,' his phone call precious because of the distance, as if he was calling from Mars. 'How is Bubbe?' his first question.

'Oy gevalt,' his mother said. 'It's too awful to talk.' Levi thought the worst; that his grandmother was dead and it was all his fault. Deena came back on the phone. 'She's taken to walking the streets at night in her underclothes,' she said. 'Mameh's distraught, dying of shame.' Deena lowered her voice. 'But Bubbe doesn't know what she's doing. It's not like she's doing it on purpose, you know? Seems like she's enjoying herself.'

The Blue Ruin Café

Mammy was doing her moustache again, the smell of the beeswax strong, steam curling off the pot. She was fierce obsessed with hair removal; it was the second time in a week. The counter at the front of the café had turned messy with her things, the gummy tubs of wax mixed up with the dusty sweet jars, the wooden spatulas sprouting from the cup meant for coffee stirrers. 'With a bit of luck you won't need to do this,' she said as she spread the golden solution over her top lip. She checked her reflection in the mirrored Coca-Cola sign hung on the tongue-and-groove, pressing a strip of gauze onto her mouth before the liquid hardened. 'See me, I'm Sicilian. Covered in hair I don't want, like the Turks, the Greek. But you're Irish, Majella, and that's as Caucasian as it gets. It only takes two generations to assimilate. That's what your old Nonno told me when you were born. "You're Irish now, Bonfilia. An Irish bambina to prove it."' She pointed the spatula at me. 'But you didn't turn me blonde now, did ye?'

My Nonno was sitting at the back of the room, at the booth nearest the window. He got up at four o'clock every morning, dressed in his Y-fronts and an inside-out woollen cardigan, and went and sat there in the café. He'd stay put until eight in the evening, eating malted biscuits and smelling of pee, the way that ninety-year-olds do. Sometimes he acted the maggot; shouting at people who weren't there, throwing his arms about in a rage. Mammy said he was reliving his days in the Italian Navy, fighting the Spanish Civil War. He didn't pay any attention to us because in his loo-la head we weren't born yet. We didn't pay much attention to him either, which is why we failed to notice he'd suffered his second stroke a week ago.

'Youch,' Mammy squealed, pulling the gauze from her lip. And at the same time there was another sound, a brazen clanging from the door chime. A fierce tall feller with yellow hair like Shaggy out of Scooby-Doo was standing in the gangway, his Barbour jacket dripping, a soggy cardboard folder under his arm. 'Bout ye?' Mammy said, eyeing him suspiciously as she wiped a gobbet of blood from her mouth.

'Could I get a coffee?' he asked scrabbling around in his pocket, coins jingling.

'Sure ye can,' Mammy said. But she didn't get up from where she was sitting. Instead she stared into his face, like an optician looking for the onset of a cataract.

'Say, you wouldn't mind if I set up in that little booth of yours over there?' he said waving at the seats at the back of the café. He was a Yank, I was sure of it. He took his folder from under his arm and showed it to Mammy, but there was nothing about its plain beige cover to signify what was inside. 'I'm the writer in residence at Queen's University this semester,' he said, explaining himself. 'It's kinda busy this time of year and I've got me a novel to finish. You won't even know I'm here.'

'You're sure you're not a reporter now?' Mammy said, her voice sluggish from her morning medication. 'I thought ye had to be dead to be a novelist, and you're a good two miles away from the University, so you are.'

'I've been looking for somewhere quiet,' he said blushing a wee bit.

She nodded at the seats at the back. 'Ah, go on with ye,' she said.

So your man put a few coins on the counter next to the waxing strips and shuffled to the other end of the café. Ach, I thought he was terrible brave to come all this way, and through Sandy Row as well. We hadn't got a real, paying customer for four months, not since the insurance money had come through on the MacDermott's chip shop and they'd turned it to a coffee house called CU Latte. 'What do they know about coffee?' Mammy'd said, 'little girls playing waitresses with their eejit plastic nametags and their skirts hitched up to here.' She'd bitten down on the pendant of her necklace, denting it between the N and the F. 'They should be so lucky getting a wee bit of shrapnel through their window. If I had that kind of money I'd be away to America now.'

It was different in the Seventies. Then the tourists would drive all the way from Bangor to buy my Nonna's vanilla pokes. Nonna was deadly with the ice-cream. Our café got its name from the colour of her eyes. My grandfather had been painting the kitchen walls at the time. He held the swatch up to her face and chose the shade that matched them best: Blue Ruin, a light electric blue, like old gin. Mammy says it's unlucky and that she'll change it the first chance she gets, but Nonno didn't know what it meant; his English wasn't all that grand back then. I never saw Nonna's eyes myself because she died two days before I was born. In the pictures they look like they have no colour at all, white like the ivory statue of the mother of God in St Peter's cathedral; she looks like she was blind.

Nonna tried to teach Mammy all about the ice-cream pokes; how to use whole milk instead of butterfat but Mammy's got the patience of the devil and only my Da picked it up. My Da died on the day of my third birthday party, kidnapped and murdered by the leader of the Shankhill Butchers on his way to buy plastic knives and forks from the cash & carry on Linfield Road. The policemen found him two days later behind a house on the Shankhill Estate. Mammy told me that he wasn't looking where he was going and got run over by a bus. I found out she was lying when at the wake I heard a drunken old feller going on about Da's coffin being screwed closed on account of his mutilated body. That's about the time Mammy developed a taste for the tranquilisers and the hair removal. Back then she liked the crossword puzzles too. She'd have a stack of them piled on the counter next to her, a pen poised behind her ear. One time when she was in the lavvy I took a peek at the one she'd left out and saw that she'd done it all wrong. Instead of answering the clues she'd written my Da's name over and over, in every grid that it would fit. Even I knew that 'Eurasian plant with fragrant white flowers (5,7)' was not a Tommy O'Keeffe.

'Would you make yer man there a nice cup of coffee now, Majella?' Mammy said. Having not seen a paying customer for so long, shyness had pushed me behind the counter where I could watch events through the grimy glass of the catering display. 'Coffee?' I said.

'Aye, coffee,' she said. 'Go on there wean, don't be bold.' She knew full well that the cappuccino machine was banjaxed, but she only winked at me and went back to her reflection in the mirror. After a few minutes, wondering what to do, I took my plastic tea set out of my toy box. It was grand I tell you – red with white polka dots and shiny, but chewed a wee bit 'round the rims. I pretended to brew the coffee into one of the cups, making the sucking sound of the old frothing nozzle by pressing my tongue against the roof of my mouth. When it was done I carried it to your Yankee feller, the way that Mammy'd taught me: slow so as not to tip any on the mosaic floor, and curtsying a wee bit as you place it fierce gentle on the table. Mammy'd been teaching me a lot now since I was off school because of the start of the marching season. There wasn't all that much to do except watch the way she served scald to Mrs. Lynch from the neighbourhood watch, or listen to the way her voice rose or fell depending on which pills she'd taken.

The man curled his lip at my plastic teacup. If he'd tried to pick it up he would have got his index finger jammed in the handle for sure. He looked past me, hoping for some assistance from my mother but she was asleep now, her tangled black hair fanned over the Formica. 'Go on sir, it's rude not to,' I said pleading with him to drink from the toy cup, the way I did with customers when I was in the low babies. But I was seven now, a big girl, and my heart wasn't in it no more. He was about to stand up when my grandfather cried out.

'Don't-a you move you asshole,' said Nonno in his thick eyetie accent, fashioning his arm into a gun, cocking two fingers and training them on the Bobby Sands mural painted on the pine end outside. There was a trickle of white saliva hanging from the corner of his grey mouth. 'Area out of bounds, rapporto to Corvette Captain.'

'Catch yourself on now, Nonno!' I said, embarrassed, and thank God he did, closing his mouth-hole and prodding at his biscuits with his fingertip. Turning to your Shaggy Rogers, I said, 'Don't mind him sir, he's playing soldiers. He's away in the head, so.' Your man there just nodded and began to fill his big notepad with narrow rows of wobbly double-writing, his head bowed over the page, as if nothing had happened. I leant over his shoulder for a minute, watching, then dandered back to the catering display, and my collection of Barbie dolls piled inside. I chose Peaches 'N Cream to play with. She was the only one left with two whole eyes. I'd gouged most of the others out. 'Bout ye, Peaches?' I said lifting her from the stale slab of Battenberg I'd been using for a mattress.

'Hey Majella,' she said. 'Yous look deadly today.'

'I know aye,' I said, crouching down low where Shaggy

couldn't see me. 'I pinched a lippy from me Mammy's handbag, so I did. Whisht now.' I put my finger to my lips and whispered, 'Do you know that that American man over there's writing a book? Aye! A whole book about a wee blonde girl who drowns in a vat of green pea soup.'

'Ach, whisht yourself Majella,' she said looking at me like I was a gobshite. 'He is not writing a book about that. He's writing a book about a man who gets his throat slit like a pig. There's going to be a picture of him on the cover too, his head lolling about like a flag on a pole. He looks like your Da, so he does.'

'He is not,' I said tightening her peach stoal around her neck and making her splutter. 'He's writing a book about a man whose stomach ruptures from eating too much of me old Nonna's vanilla pokes. They were deadly, they were. He couldn't stop himself.'

Peaches flashed her brilliant white teeth at me like a rabid dog. 'No he is not,' she said. 'He's writing a book about your Nonno and all the cack he talks, the sky pilot that he is. Look at your man over there, studying the old fella as we talk.'

It was dark before he was away, his notebook full to brimming, and Mammy was awake again, her face in the Coca-Cola mirror, a pair of tweezers prised in her hand. 'That's you, is it?' she said as he tried to sidle past unnoticed. He stopped, snickering self-consciously. Mammy smiled at him, the tweezers left open in mid air as if waiting to catch a fly. 'Are ye ever going to tell us what you're writing about now?' she said arching her back like a cat.

'It's a secret,' your man said, fidgeting with his folder.
'Is it now?' Mammy said. 'We'll see about that then.'

Sure enough Shaggy was back the next day with a
Thermos flask and a round of peanut butter sandwiches
wrapped in tin foil. He came every day that spring,
sitting in the same place across from my grandfather,
scribbling frenziedly on his foolscap notepad. Slowly but
surely, Mammy came back to life, combing snarls out of
her hair instead of dozing through whole afternoons. One
day, early in May, she dusted the tops of the sweet jars
on the floating shelf. She made Rice Krispies cakes.
'Would yous tell us what your book is about already?'
she said, sighing, as Shaggy packed his things up one
evening.

'It's kinda boring actually,' your man said, shaking his
head, 'The 1946 Greek Civil War. You see? It's boring,
and the reason I didn't tell you first off.'

'Oh aye,' Mammy said. 'War. That's a bore so it is. I'd
rather French kiss a barracuda than read that shite.
Why'd ye want ta write it anyway? Would ye take me
Daddy over there, babbling away, senile as the devil?
They say he's gone back to his best days, doing
Mussolini's dirty work. Nobody would think he had a
wife or a daughter or a grandbaby. Wait till I tell ye, I
lost my husband in the war, so I did.' She pushed the
cuticle on her index finger down with her wee wooden
stick. It was the most she'd said in four years.

'What war?' yer man said, his elbow on the counter.

'What war?' Mammy said mocking him. She pointed
at the row of great boulders lining the pavement outside.
'This one, yer eejit.'

'Of course,' he said. 'I'm sorry.'

'You're alright,' she said, her voice fierce breathy, like she was having an asthma attack. 'But you should write about something happy, a love story, so.' Their faces were close, their noses nearly touching. 'I'm going away for a couple of weeks now,' the man said pulling back. 'Home to the US for an engagement, but I'll be back real soon. I'll bring you a little something.'

The next day my Nonno was dead, his face a quare mixture of shock and composure. I tried to feed him his favourite biscuits but his lips were blue and stiff. I took my Pop Singer Mitzi doll to his funeral a few days later. To be fair she was a Sindy, and not a Barbie, but she was the only doll wearing a black dress. She gurned through the whole ceremony about my leaving her wee plastic microphone in the catering display. 'It's my trademark, Majella, you dumb ape yer. I never leave home without it.' In the car, going through Milltown Cemetery, she eyed the big Celtic cross gravestones and groaned, tears in her eyes. 'Won't be long before I'm here myself so,' she said. 'Stuck in that filthy café with that slob of a Mammy of yours, I'll starve to death before long for sure! How'll I ever be a real pop star like your woman Madonna, Majella? How'll I ever make it in America and play the Hollywood Bowl?' I got pretty cheesed off with her whining, truth be told, so I shoved her head-first into Mrs. Lynch's patent handbag.

By the time your man Shaggy Rogers came back from America, Mammy was back to her old ways, napping on the counter. She was dead to the world when he walked in late on a Monday morning, a gift-wrapped box under his arm. He looked a right Dicky Dazzler in a new linen suit and all. He glanced about in search of my grandfather. 'He's dead, so he is,' I said.

He nodded sympathetically. 'I'm not sitting down today,' he said. 'I just came to drop this off.' He put the box on the counter next to my Mammy's head.

'What is it?' I asked.

'It's just a little something, Honey, for your mother's American customers. It's my favourite.' He reached out, gently shaking Mammy's wrist.

'Mammy!' I cried, trying to rouse her, but she never did listen to me. She was out cold. 'I have to go,' the man said, his voice sad. 'Will you tell her I'll see her around?'

'You don't have to go yet,' I said. I untwisted the lid on one of the sweet jars. 'Have some Parma Violets. They're good for your brain to be sure, or take a black Jack. When you eat them your tongue goes blue, like when you swear but you don't even need to swear, so you don't.'

'Not today, thanks,' he said. He began to walk away, the material of his suit making a snazzy swishing sound. As the door chimes jangled after him I caught sight of the dolls on my old Nonna's cake stand, Mitzi lying down knackered and dying. I ran out into the street, scanning it for the man's yellow Shaggy hair. At the end of the block he was waiting at the zebra crossing, his bottom lip sucked into his mouth. 'Here be's me,' I said, pulling on his trouser leg. He kneeled down to be level with me. 'I've got this friend who's a singer,' I said. 'She wants to go to California and make it big. You could take her there, couldn't ya? You're from America.'

'From Chicago, yeah,' he said. 'It's a fair old way to California.'

'It's near enough,' I said, frowning a wee bit.

He smiled at me. 'I guess it is.'

'Come on with ye, then,' I said, grabbing at his hand. 'She's back at the café. I'll introduce ye.' Your man there checked his watch and straightened up slowly, looking this way and that. 'Would ye hurry the devil up?' I said. 'It's a matter of life an' death, I tell ye.'

'OK, OK,' he said.

As we got back to the door of the Blue Ruin I could see Mammy, awake and picking at the crusts in the corners of her eyes. 'There ye are,' she said as we stepped inside. She curled her lip at the glass jar on the counter, the gift wrap strewn about. 'Maple syrup?' she said to your man, her voice playful. 'Last of the big spenders, aye, and don't yer think I'm sweet enough?' She took a big gulp of air and licked around her lips. 'Anyway I'm glad you're back, so,' she said. 'You can help me think up a new name for this place, you a real writer an' all.'

The Family Yang

We carry the casket on our shoulders, stopping intermittently, changing direction in order to confuse the spiteful spirits that linger around the newly dead. My fourteen-year-old daughter, Mai, guides our procession around the neighbourhood, the flame of the tiki torch jejune in the daylight. The reed pipe is sublime, but amiss in a place like this. For a moment we expect the delicate, wavering tune to melt the hard macadam, to crush the brick suburbs, to alter the ash trees lining the sidewalk. We expect the new world to shape-shift into the Laos mountaintops: nutrient-rich ochre soil sprouting split bamboo and elephant grass. The cul-de-sac remains its cold gravel and concrete self, as unremarkable and unfamiliar as the day we arrived ten months ago, the metal mail boxes enveloped in the season's first sprinkling of snow.

Reluctantly we hand the corpse of my friend and clan

brother, Thaying Chai, to the American funeral directors for transportation to the cemetery. At his grave overlooking the city we line up, all fifty-three of us, taking turns to pick stones from a bucket and place them down at the edge of his resting place. Mai has wandered over to a wooden fence, ten yards away. She is gathering handfuls of the copper-coloured leaves fallen from the maple trees. She stuffs them – pile after pile – into the pockets of her traditional flower-cloth dress, their brown and watery secretions staining the white fabric. My wife, Mee, notices this and hisses at our daughter. 'Mai! Get back here now!' She tries to lure her back to the line with a curled and beckoning hand. Mai approaches slowly, stomping heavily on the grass, her mouth pursed and sour. Mee turns to me, her thin smile quivering, threatening to disappear. But in less than a second it is restored. Anger and sadness is not acceptable at a Hmong funeral, especially not this one.

Our clan brother, Thaying, was taken two nights ago by the malign jealous-woman spirit, Dab tsuam. Dab tsuam has been busy. In the last month she has suffocated five Hmong men in Wisconsin. Now it seems she's drifted west and chosen our clan, the Hmong Der of Minneapolis, to be her next victim. Of course, I am no stranger to her deeds. She struck many, many times in the old countries: when I was only a young Lao Sung boy she dropped by our small township, taking fifteen men in two weeks. The farmers became so anxious they began dressing as women, borrowing their wives' and mothers' skirts and headdresses. I saw my own father wear my mother's beads draped around his neck to go to bed. The

Americans will not acknowledge the existence of Dab tsuam. They say the deaths are down to a mysterious phenomenon called Sudden Unexpected Nocturnal Death Syndrome. They insist on performing post-mortems on our clan brothers' bodies, an abomination to Hmong culture. Everybody knows that when you cut a person's skin, the spirits swoop inside. And so it is imperative that this funeral is conducted in the precise manner, that the Family Yang stand together to protect Thaying from evil. Then, if the gods are willing, his three souls will fly to their rightful places: the first will be born in Laos, the land of his ancestors; the second will stay at the grave, while the third will remain in the presence of his descendants, guiding them safely through their own lives.

Back at our house, Mee, Mia and my ten-year-old son, Toua, eat their dinner on the card table in the kitchen. Satiated, I sit on the rocking chair on the porch watching a red sunset. Soon the long, bitter winter will begin. It was the middle of November when we arrived in this country; the chill on the wind enough to freeze the hair on our chins. Our sponsors told us that this temperature was normal. They gave us gifts of woollen hats and padded gloves. We didn't think we'd make it to spring without the cold solidifying us, turning us to statues on the sidewalk. We were a people used only to heat. For long hours we sat at the window watching the snow pile up, convinced its sheer volume would bury us alive.

'Gnia! Gnia?' Mee calls my name, her voice shrill with turmoil. I pull the mesh screen back to find Toua rolling on the floor, his skin white as goat milk, eyes rolling back into his head. His body is convulsing, jerking in irregular fits and starts. Mee and Mai are standing over him, hands covering their mouths.

'A gift,' I tell them. The mountain shaman of Laos jittered and writhed in much the same manner whilst summoning fortune from the gods. 'He is growing into a shaman. A shaman! My first-born son!'

'He's ill,' Mai says, glowering. 'Can you not see that he is seriously ill?'

Mee tries to soothe our daughter, smoothing her shoulder blades through her woollen sweater. 'Your father says it's a good thing.' Mai brushes her mother away, slapping hysterically. She runs to the telephone in the hall. The telephone is a dusty avocado green contraption intended to aid contact between clan members – large groups of us have been distributed all across the twin cities – sometimes months go by without visits, especially in winter. It was a gift from the Hmong elders but The Family Yang has not used it yet. I worry that it's a cruel American trick, a device the government is employing to monitor our private lives. Sometimes when I am alone in the house I lift the receiver and listen to the strange purring noise inside the machine, and then quickly replace it, spooked. 'I'm calling 911,' Mai says, herself lifting the receiver. She stabs her finger into one of the holes at the front, dragging the plastic wheel anti-clockwise. 'Toua is seriously ill. Toua's dying.'

The ambulance arrives, its sonorous whew-whew-whew announcing our troubles to our American neighbours in the clapboards around us. They stand in their windows, gawping, as two white men burst into our house, barking in a language that only Mai can understand. One of them holds Toua's head while the other inserts a metal tool into his mouth. 'A tongue retainer,' Mai says, translating, 'to prevent him biting his tongue.'

'Stop them,' I yell. 'Make them stop right now!' Touching a child's head is anathema – the soul resides in a person's head, interfering with it is as wrong as a fire ablaze underwater, a tree growing upside down. Mee cries as the men strap our son into a stretcher, her throat full of a terrific gargling noise, a life all of its own. They bundle him into the back of the vehicle, leaving as quickly and as noisily as they arrived. 'The Emergency Room,' Mai explains. 'We can follow if we can get a ride.' She goes to the telephone again – twice in one day – and contacts her dab laug, her maternal uncle. He owns a tiny green motorcar which he uses to deliver Chinese takeaway food. He lives a few miles north.

When we arrive at ER thirty minutes later. Toua is asleep in a curtained-off section with white children. A woman with a collision of bitumen-black curls piled high up on her head talks at us in short bursts of high-pitched melody. Mai interprets quickly in the narrow spaces between each of the tuneful explosions. 'The patient is resting- The patient is stable- The patient has been sedated with a mild barbiturate- The patient will be able to go home tomorrow- The patient will need to return in a few weeks- The patient will need to be monitored- The staff will decide on a long-term treatment for the patient's disorder.'

'What disorder?' I lament. 'It's a gift, not an illness. Your brother has a gift!'

I go to Toua's bed and pull the incense sticks from my

jacket pocket. I set them down on the windowsill nearby, balancing them carefully over the edge. As I light them with a match a salvo of sandalwood scent suffuses the large open room. The woman with the mess of bitumen-black hair rushes towards them, flapping her arms like a frightened chicken. She kicks the sticks to the floor, stamping on them, extinguishing them. 'We're close to the respiratory area, father,' Mai says. 'The smoke will damage the other patients' breathing.' My daughter is speaking for herself now. She has switched allegiances. She's in cahoots with the American. 'Sandalwood,' I tell her, though she already knows. 'It has healing properties. It will help.'

'Father? Please?' She has raised her voice, something no good Hmong daughter would ever do. 'We are not in the hills anymore!'

'You think I don't know that?' I ask her. 'Was it my choice to leave? The hill people give their everything to the American, and this is how they're repaid. Disrespect. Ignorance. They fill my son's body with poison. They mutilate the bodies of my clan brothers.' I pinch at the bridge of my nose, asking the spirits to alleviate the pain in my soul. 'They turn my own daughter against me.'

I was a young man, newly married, on the day I first encountered an American soldier. It was February 1967, twenty-one years ago. I was up on the mountain tending to the opium field when I first noticed him in the distance, crouched on his hands and knees, side-winding through the poppies like a crocodile, stalks shifting this way and that. I spied around, looking for my father, but he had already worked his way over to the adjacent field, an acre away. As the soldier got closer he rose up on his knees. He was tall, and armed with a sophisticated weapon. He beckoned me, speaking in a shaky Mong Leng dialect. 'Friend,' he said, poking at his sternum. 'Don't be afraid of me. I come in peace.' I could not take my eyes off his thick, curly hair, the colour and texture of pampas grass, or his round blue eyes, like holes filled with clear sky. I looked from his eyes to his hair to his eyes to his hair to his eyes and back again.

Within a month all the Lao Sung farmers in the area were working for the soldiers, blocking the Ho Chi Minh Trail in exchange of money and an abundance of food. Once a week the soldiers arrived with cases of fresh red meat, whole carcasses of cattle and swine, enough to feed the villagers four times over. We learned to regard the white man as a comrade, so much so that later in the same year, my clan brother Xang and I saved a downed American pilot from an ambush of tigers, carrying him on a bamboo stretcher from the eastern jungle all the way to the military base in Long Cheng. They tried to build a helicopter pad on the precipice of the magic cave, where the Toj Phim Nyaj – the guardian of the mountain – resided. It was untouched by humans, surrounded by monkeys and tigers, and they had to give up half way through because the soldiers were struck down with unexplained nausea and nosebleeds. Eventually they used dynamite to clear the area and the guardian of the mountain was killed. Even then we trusted them to protect and feed us.

In 1970 the Americans ceased operations and we found ourselves back in the poppy fields. Our involvement in their war remained a secret in the west, but the North Vietnamese Army knew of our exploits. When they overthrew our country two years later, they immediately retaliated. Hordes of communist forces attacked the hills, capturing men and raping women. My father went missing from his bed one night. Two days later, whilst chasing a troop of monkeys back to the jungle, Mai and Toua found his body in a shallow ravine, his throat slit. It was then that we decided to flee, leaving our hut and trekking for ten days over the border into Thailand. Along the way we encountered many emptied villages, huts left the same way as ours, dinner plates on the table, clothing hung in the sunshine to dry. Mee, tired of carrying both children, begged to stop and rest awhile in the abandoned bamboo-woven beds. It was too dangerous. Often we passed by the corpses of hill people, half eaten by animals or killed and dismembered by soldiers. When we rested it was in brief snatches, hidden under elephant grass, one of us staying awake to keep watch over the others. We almost lost Toua in the Mekong River when Mee stepped on a sea cow, dropping him into the current. Finally we arrived at a squalid refugee camp, our feet and hands grazed and bleeding. We lived there with hundreds of other Hmong families for a total of thirteen years, relying always on the kindness of strangers, our bellies rumbling so that often they were louder than the bamboo pipes we played to pass the time. The American charity workers arrived every three or four months, taught some of the older children a little of their language then left again taking fifty or sixty people away with them. Towards the end of 1987 they took us finally, depositing us here in the USA.

Six o'clock on a bleak October evening the carpool drops me at our cul-de-sac, knuckles sore from a shift at the food-packaging plant. Toua is standing in the hallway facing the wall, his schoolbag at his feet. Without noticing my arrival he proceeds to hit his forehead against the wall, over and over again, the noise a low thud that reverberates along the picture rail.

'Boy,' I say, alerting him to my presence.

He stops, looking up at me, eyes blank and unseeing. He turns back to the wall, continuing with his destructive, repellent behaviour. Something about it makes me want to slap his chest. 'Boy! Don't do that!' I tell him. I lift him by his armpits, carrying him to the card table where Mai is sitting, the dead leaves she collected from the cemetery set out in front of her. She picks one, sticking it with a thin layer of glue to a page in her schoolbook. Mee is standing at the stove, stirring vegetables in the new wok her brother gave her. I sit down opposite Mai, positioning the boy in my lap. 'Why are you hurting yourself?' I ask him, my arms clenched around his waist. 'You are battling with demons?'

Mai snorts at the suggestion without looking up from her book.

Toua wriggles, trying to fight free. 'Why?' I ask him, gripping tighter.

'The only demons here are the Americans,' Toua blurts, resigned to my strength. 'I can't understand anything they say. I'm a dummy. Everyday I sit in their classroom like a dummy. They ask me questions. I don't know what they're asking. The only word I know is no. "Do I want something?" No! "Do I want to eat?" No! "Do I want to go outside?" No! Everyday. No. No. No.' His voice cracks, a sob rattling between his tiny ribs. 'I am so lonely, father. I want to go back to the camp in Thailand. At least there they spoke our language.'

'You are not a dummy,' I tell my son. 'You have extraordinary gifts. You're a special, special little man.'

Mai glares at me over her pen, the same disapproving look I get from her mother when I eat too much broiled pork. She is already a woman. If we'd stayed in Laos she would be married by now. She would have a husband to keep her in line. 'Get real, father,' she says. 'He's not gifted. He's ill.' Her eyes bug out defiantly. 'He can't learn anything because he has a constant headache. The other children are way ahead of him. Don't you get it? There is no magic in America.'

Mee turns from the wok, whipping Mai with a towel. 'Girl! Do not speak to your father like that. You turn as ugly as a cave rat when you insult your parents so. Help me with the dishes.'

Mai raises her arms to protect herself from the whipping. 'No,' she says flatly. 'Why should I do the dishes? The other girls at my school don't do dishes.' She thumps at the table, a leaf crumbling under her fist. 'American families have dishwashers. We don't have one because we're freaks. My own father is so stupid he believes in spirits and magic.' Looking at her brother she says, 'You are a dummy, Toua. You always will be if you listen to him.'

I stand up, Toua sliding from my lap. 'You'll listen to

me you American punk!' I take hold of Mai's wrist and drag her out of her chair and towards the door, the pen in her hand dropping and clattering on the table's surface. Mee catches my eye in the process. 'The woman from Wisconsin,' she reminds me. Rumour has it that a Hmong mother has been prosecuted for slapping her daughter's hand. There are laws in this country that say we cannot punish our children. In the mountains we would beat them with the carpet stick, once for insolence, ten times for stealing. Mai's arm slips out of my fingers as if they're coated in butter.

'That's right,' she says, a smirk on her mouth, her eyes not quite meeting mine. 'You can't touch me.' She throws herself down on her chair and takes the pen, as if to sign a final severance. Her hand hovers and then slams down on the page. 'The other girls get paid to do chores,' she says. 'If I'm going to spend half my life washing dishes then I want payment. I want a pair of roller skates.'

'Roller skates,' I repeat the word, startled.

Toua knocks his head against the table leg from where he sits cross-legged on the floor. Seedlings of panic begin to sprout beneath my skin.

'We'll get you the roller skates,' Mee says, 'if you teach your brother to speak English.'

Mai looks sideways at me, lips pursed. I nod. 'If you are so good at being American, teach your brother, and you'll be rewarded.'

'Really?' says Mai.

'Yes.' Mee whips her with the towel one more time. 'Now, help me with the dishes.' Mai is on the cusp of pushing her chair back and getting up to aid her mother.

Then her face becomes paralysed, expression stuck somewhere between indignation and pride. Staring over my shoulder, her mouth flaps open and closed a few times before finally shaping itself around two stuttering words. 'Mr. Moua?' she says.

The Hmong elder responsible for our cul-de-sac is standing in the kitchen doorway wearing his traditional silk sashes and coin purse. 'I'm sorry,' he says, bowing gingerly. 'The front door was open.' My face burns red as I realise that he's witnessed some, or all of Mai's fearsome behaviour. 'I bring news,' he says. 'Bad news, I'm afraid. Dab tsuam has struck again. Tai Cheng, a fellow from the cutting area at your plant, was found dead this morning. The funeral begins at his house in North Frogtown tomorrow.'

By the beginning of the New Year celebrations we have lost four Hmong men in the Cities area. 'A terrible affair,' my friend and clan brother, Neng Po says. 'We are safe nowhere. Even to the new world she follows us.' He shakes his head and turns to watch the teenagers playing pov pob in the living room. Their cheering is so clamorous it's impossible to continue with our own adult conversation. A Mong Leng girl wearing her clan-customary pleated skirt launches the ball a little too forcefully, knocking Mee's lucky wax elephant off the bookshelf. I sigh and take another sip of my rice liquor. The rice liquor is particularly palatable this year, strong and fiery, giving me a warm, convivial feeling in my belly. Already Neng Po and I have consumed two whole bottles. We've been drinking steadily all day long, a little here, a little there, enough to keep us consistently hooked up to a slight buzz, every sip like throwing meat to the wolf at the door. Now the second bottle is empty. 'Mee!' I yell, calling for a third.

'Take it easy,' she says when she arrives, bashing the bottle down on our side table. 'You'll make yourselves sick.'

'Come, come woman,' I snap as she walks away. 'It's New Year! A celebration! Did you forget it was New Year, you bad-tempered woman?' I refill our little glasses to the top. 'Bottoms up, brother,' I say, instructing Neng to drink.

Less than an hour later I can feel the liquor, like lead in my blood. My body's heavy, buckled in the kitchen chair. I can hardly lift my head as Neng insists on pouring another large measure. 'Down the hatch!' he says clinking his glass against mine. 'Call back the wandering souls to unite.' He swallows his drink and waits for me to do the same. Somehow I manage it all in one gulp. But now I need the bathroom. 'Excuse me,' I say standing and heading for the staircase, the floor underneath me as rocky as a rudderless junk. I am sure that I'm going to vomit. There seems to be a pool of gelatinous liquid gathered at the root of my oesophagus. But on the landing I am inexplicably drawn to the spectacle of my king size bed. As I curl up on it I decide that there is one good thing about America after all. Yes, the children are wicked, the women sullen, the white man ignorant, but the mattresses are filled with wool.

An indefinite amount of time has passed before I realise that I am not on the bed. In fact I am soaring in the air, my body planate, one arm outstretched, like

Superman in flight. I'm outside, above the houses, venturing eastward through patches of cold, cirra-cumulus cloud. I'm travelling quickly, over mountains and lakes, rivers and oceans, the waters colourless, pastures frost-tinged and blue. The further I travel, the warmer it becomes, the toy-like landscapes below me turning yellow and sandy, my clothes dripping from my body in fragments, my arms morphing to wings. I try a somersault, testing gravity: I am weightless, unfettered by law or geography. I call out in search of other travellers but am answered only by the high-pitched song of a treecreeper flying at a lower altitude to me.

Soon I encounter the opium fields and rice paddies of Laos; the terraces carved into the mountainside, the older men, stick figures, working them like ants. My father is here. So is the guardian of the mountain's cave, a troop of playful monkeys clinging to the edges of its dark mouth, the treasure and jewellery inside glinting cockily in the sun. This is the Laos of my childhood.

'Gnia!' I hear a faint voice from a far-off place: another world. I snap my head from side to side, searching for its source. All I see are the coolie hats of the men working the fields. Soon I will land in my own family's field. I can see it clearly; the poppies fat and ready to be harvested.

'Gnia, wake up. You're having a nightmare. Wake up.'

I open my eyes. I see the ugly face of the Dab tsuam, the whites of her eyes wet and shining in the light of the moon. I scream and wrestle but she is sitting on my belly, holding me down. 'Gnia!' she says, slapping at my face. 'Wake up, Gnia. It's me; it's Mee. What the heck is the matter with you?'

During the long, joyless days of January when the arctic temperatures prevent any kind of socialising, I sometimes wish that my wife had let me go back to the land of my ancestors. Gelid minutes seem to last for hours, the second hand of the clock ticking, lonesome as a rabid dog. The sidewalks are frozen and empty, commuters taken to the overhead corridors to avoid the hypothermia promised by the winter in the Midwest plains. Merely peeking out of the window will cause a bout of depression or a brief spell of snow-blindness. Ravens perch on the telegraph wires, glaciated lumps of black feather. At a drop in the temperature they plummet to the ground, solid and dead as rocks. Late one battleship-grey morning, our Hmong elder, Mr. Moua visits the food packaging plant. We place our knives down on the workbench and adjust our hairnets as he enters. 'Brothers, I bring news,' he says, bowing carefully. We suspect the worst. 'It seems we have been bestowed with two thousand square yards of land in a place called Corcoran in the southernmost area of the city. This land is to be used as a community garden. It will be shared equally among you, and there you can grow produce to sell at the annual farmer's market.'

Neng Po, ecstatic with the announcement, beckons us into a small huddle next to the factory wall, suggesting we offer our lunchboxes to Mr. Moua, honouring him the way we do Xim Kaab, the god of wealth. Mr. Moua laughs benignly at us, waving our kindness away. 'It's a gift from the American people,' he says. 'Not from me.' And suddenly we understand why this land is so far away. It will be a stinking swamp, unfit for use by the Americans and therefore unfit for us: an albatross dressed up as philanthropy; more of their evil tricks.

At the weekend I have to take my son to his appointment at the hospital. The children's dab lang is at work, delivering takeaways – winter is a busy time for the takeaway industry since nobody wants to leave their house to go to a restaurant or even to the store to buy groceries – we have to use public transport. We wait at the bus stop at the end of the avenue, dressed like the Inuit peoples of Alaska. Often we are mistaken by the white man for the Inuit peoples of Alaska, but more often we are mistaken for Vietnamese refugees, a disastrous error which almost always results in our getting spat on. The bus – a winding, metal caterpillar – arrives with a puff and we climb aboard. 'Thank you,' Toua says in English as the driver hands our change back to us, his face hidden behind a thick fur-lined hood.

'You see?' I say nudging my son as we head to a seat near the radiator. 'You are not a dummy.'

'It's just one word,' he says, shrugging my compliment off, embarrassed.

When we arrive at the hospital lobby we are greeted by a young, enthusiastic Asian woman, her hair tied in a sleek knot held together with coral pins. At a guess I would plump for Chinese, our oldest enemy. 'Toua?' she says, her voice breathy with solicitude as she stoops to shake my son's hand. 'Who are you?' I ask her abruptly in Hmong Daw, stamping the snow off my boots, not expecting her to understand.

'I'm Kia,' she says, straightening up. 'Kia Hang. I started here last week. Moved up from the San Joaquin Valley in California.' She speaks an uncluttered mix of Hmong Shua and Miao. She offers me her hand, and I take it, numbed with shock. 'I am not a medical professional,' she says. 'Just an interpreter. I speak Hmong, many dialects, so I'll be able to explain everything the nurses have to say.' She blinks a few times, waiting for a reply. 'We'll take it,' I think, though I say nothing, my larynx petrified with gratitude. She points over at the doors of the elevator and smiles. 'Shall we?' she says.

When we're done at the hospital, Toua and I take a second bus, a southern route, heading toward the dubious community garden in Corcoran. 'Are you sure I'm going to be all right?' Toua says, reaching for my hand as we alight from the bus. His fingers are cold, and smaller than I expected. In a place like America, where the children grow so hellishly fast it's easy to forget that they are the children; that you are the adult. 'Of course you will,' I assure him. 'You heard what Kia said. With the right medication you can live a normal life. Your headaches will disappear.' I repeat the hand gesture Kia acted so deftly in the office of the children's ward, a lightning-quick, open-handed wave. 'Whoosh. Vanished. As swift as a ghost monkey.'

We are nearing the white wrought-iron gates of the garden, one of them flapping a little in the wind. 'But father?' Toua says. 'When the headaches go will you still think I'm special?'

Without analysing his question I answer him honestly.

'Of course you are special, Toua. You are my first-born son!'

We are not the first to arrive at the garden; that is certain. Much of the ground has already been sectioned off, the various names of my clan brothers written on placards and jammed into the hard earth. There is one patch, an eight by eight foot rectangle, nestled between Neng Po and someone called Chai Cheng. I was hoping for an end plot, but have no choice. I look around for a few minutes, gauging the mood of the location. The garden is flanked on one side by a lonely cornfield, and on the other by an office block, stick figures rushing around inside. It's silent save for the muted hiss of the traffic on the intersection a mile away. It's too cold for clouds, the sun dazzling and terrible. 'It's not so bad, huh?' I ask Toua who grunts incuriously, rubbing his hands together. I kneel down at the edge of our newly claimed patch, combing the soil through my fingers until it turns soft and moist, the warm telluric smell of it gently opening my nostrils. For the first time since New Year I feel properly alive. 'Look here,' I say to him, pulling a bunched napkin from my coat pocket.

'What is it?' he asks.

I show him the seeds I've been germinating on our kitchen windowsill. 'Chilli peppers, boy.' I have him press the seeds into the earth, hunks of the dirt clinging to his glowing red fingertips. Together we cover the seeds, patting the earth above them flat and smooth. 'By summer we will have good, red juicy chilli peppers,' I say. 'Who says there's no magic in America, huh?'

The yelling from the kitchen is audible from the stoop

as early that evening we arrive back at the house. Mee and Mai are standing on opposite sides of the card table, a cardboard box opened between them. Inside, resting on layers of tissue paper is a pair of blue suede roller skates, embellished with strips of red and yellow leather. 'Roller skates!' I say, remembering their name. 'Someone's a lucky girl today.'

'Not me!' Mai pouts. 'The one who gave them away. I am the laughing stock of the whole neighbourhood; the Hmong girl with the American's cast-offs.' I frown at her, perplexed. 'Are you blind, father?' she screams, pointing into the box. 'The stoppers are scuffed. Look at them.' She wipes thin, angry tears from her face, huffing and struggling to catch her breath. She's right of course. The knobs of yellow plastic attached to the toes are scratched and dirt-encrusted.

'From the charity bank,' Mee explains. 'How can we afford new?'

'Other people get new,' Mai spits.

'You're not other people, Mai,' I tell her. 'You are you.'

'I hate being me,' she says. 'And I hate having parents like you.'

'So ask the spirits,' I tell her. 'Ask the spirits to look after you.'

She wrings her hands and grinds her teeth, then turns and runs upstairs to her room, stomping on every tread. 'Would you like me to dispose of them?' I call after her, teasingly. 'I can drop them in the garbage outside. You'll never have to see them again.' For a moment the house is soundless, the rafters breathing lightly, and then comes the stomping.

Mai appears before us in the kitchen. 'Thank you, mother,' she hisses in English, whipping the box from the table, securing it under her arm.

Hard as Nails

My tabard was covered in cat's hair, black needles thread through the pink cotton on the bust and the skirt and the collar. I didn't realise until I was at the end of Trinity Road and struggling to untangle my iPod wires. There was something in the herbal hand lotion at the salon that acted like catnip. Sooty went nuts for it. If I didn't hang my tabard in the wardrobe he'd roll all over it like a slug dipped in salt. Last night was yoga class: I'd thrown my uniform in a rushed heap on the bathroom floor and my mother, sick of cleaning up after me, left it there. I gave up on the iPod, ripping the buds out of my ears and stuffing it into my work bag. I was nervous already. I'd woken to a letter from the new nail salon in Pontypridd, inviting me for an interview in a week's time. I'd sent my CV on a whim, after a bad week at Hard as Nails. Joanna wasn't paying me enough in the first place, and then she'd confiscated my tips. Now I was petrified about her finding out about my trying to leave.

It was eight forty-five as I rounded the corner onto the high street, a Friday in the middle of August. The sky was curdled; the town damp-smelling. Seren had opened up. She was sitting in the backroom eating cereal, the bowl balanced between her knees. I went straight to the desk, cutting strips of Sellotape with which to prise the cat hair from my overall.

Joanna came in a little after nine, her sixteen-year-old son, Conan, in tow. He was wearing his stainless steel colander on his head, the kind that has two small handles on either side, the names of food pressed out of the sides to act as drainage: salad, pasta, fruit. He called it his 'Britney helmet', He reckoned he could communicate spiritually with Britney Spears while he was wearing it. Conan had a mental age of eleven but a memory like a camera. He'd remember things he'd heard on the telly and repeat them for months on end. 'Pain in the arse kid,' Joanna said, sending him to the armchair. 'Babysitter's let me down again.' She went to the fridge. As she opened it Seren froze, the spoon in her hand suspended in front of her O-shaped mouth. 'I knew it,' Joanna barked. 'No milk.' She slammed the door closed, the bottles of wine inside shaking. 'I'll go,' said Seren. She dropped her spoon into the dish, the milk splashing. 'I'll go. It's my fault.'

Joanna eyeballed her miserably. 'No, I will,' she said. 'You'll take too long. Put the kettle on.' Joanna turned and headed for the entrance, picking up her handbag on her way out. For a time the room was still, filled with the echo of the door chime. 'What's Britney saying today, Conan?' Seren asked, taking her spoon up. Conan tapped the colander with his knuckle. 'She's saying,' he said, pausing momentarily for effect, 'that our brains can only develop from loving relationships. She's saying that cruelly treated children grow into cruel adults who crave a lot of attention.' Seren nodded absently, slipping a spoonful of her breakfast sludge past her glossy lips. The smell of it was fresh, citrus-like. 'What is that?' I asked her. Seren was a fifteen-year-old chain-smoker. She only ate breakfast when it was doughnuts from ASDA or muffins from Maccy D's. 'Tangerine,' she said, chewing as she spoke.

'In milk?'

'Yeah.' There was a disturbance then, coming from outside, Joanna's voice crackling. We got up and stumbled to the front of the shop, all three of us hanging out of the door. Joanna had Mrs. Winterbottom pinned against the pebble-dashed wall of the bank, the tips of their noses almost touching. 'How many years?' Joanna was shouting into Mrs. Winterbottom's face, slapping the wall next to her as she uttered each word, breast heaving with rage.

'Oh, don't get so het up,' Mrs. Winterbottom said, trying to wriggle out of the acquisition. 'I told you. My daughter gave me a voucher. Under normal circumstances I would have come to you. You know that, Jo.' Joanna'd caught Mrs. Winterbottom leaving the rival nail salon on the opposite side of the street. 'How many years?' she repeated, words peppered with spittle. The optician was out at his door now too, fiddling with the lapels of his white coat.

'Two years, Joanna. Only two years you've been here.'

'Well, two years and no more,' Joanna spluttered. 'You're banned from Hard as Nails now, forever, and it's your stupid fucking daughter's fault. You want to go to American Nails? You're welcome. Piss on your own fireworks, why don't you?' She turned around, coming towards us. I couldn't help flinching as she approached: I knew that's what I had coming if she found out about my interview, worse probably. She'd butcher me. 'What are you all looking at?' she said. 'Inside! Come on!' She clapped her hands, dispersing us. 'That's it,' she said, when we were all in, the door chimes clanging. 'I've had as much as I can take. No appointments for next week so we'll shut up shop, book a self-catering cheapy, Benidorm, Alicante, wherever.'

It had been a funny time in Tonypandy since the centenary of the riots the previous year. There'd been a march through the town to mark it and the council had unveiled a statue in the car park – the Lady with the Lamp, a woman in a brown dress, the lamp balanced on her head. From a distance it looked like she was drinking a yard of ale. Afterwards everyone had congregated outside the supermarket to watch a laser show, gloved hands curled around cans of lager. Joanna was so drunk she got the heel of her best shoe caught in the gutter and had to limp home, sliding everywhere on the ice. It was a Sunday night. The salon was closed the following day. When we came back on Tuesday the boarded-up jeweller shop across the road had reopened as a nail salon. There were signboards painted with big American flags, and a neon sign in the window. Joanna had been apoplectic.

She stood on the doorstep, glaring, her keys bunched in her hand, their metal ridges cutting into the skin of her palm. 'What the fucking fuck?' she muttered to herself. 'What the fucking, fuck, fuck?' Seren made coffee and tried to hand her a mug. Joanna waved it away, eyes glazed. 'Right!' she said after half an hour. She opened the till and prised out forty pounds, forcing the money into Seren's hand. 'Get over there and ask them for a Hot Mitts manicure. Let's see what we're up against.'

Seren was out of the door more quickly than angels can fly, pausing to light a cigarette on the pavement. I had to call her back. 'Take your tabard off, Ser,' I said. 'They'll see the name of our salon on it.' She unpopped her buttons, shrugged out of her overall, and swapped it for her hoodie.

'Remember everything,' Joanna said. 'And for God's sake don't give them a bloody tip.' Joanna went back to the window to watch Seren cross the street.

'Do you think they're really American?' I asked her from the desk.

'Don't be stupid, Kayla,' she answered. 'They'll be from Maerdy, or the other valley.' I hadn't meant the technicians, but the manicures. In America they filed nails to a point; in Europe you file them square. I'd learned these things on my Beauty GNVQ. I was properly qualified, unlike Seren, whom Joanna had taken on as a favour to her cousin, Seren's mother, before Seren had sat her CSEs. Joanna was tidying her workstation, arranging the nail polish colours in alphabetical order. She moved her container full of emery boards an inch across the surface of the desk and stared at it sombrely for a moment. Then she moved it again, to the other side. She muttered something to herself before sliding it back to its original position. Our first customer arrived and I busied myself making coffee and warming towels, until Seren came back, her head swollen with the secret information, eyes watery with glee.

'Where the hell have you been?' said Joanna. 'It doesn't take that long.'

Seren stood in the middle of the salon, enjoying the attention. 'Chinks,' she spat.

'What?' Joanna curled her hair behind her ears, as if its presence in front of them had caused her to mishear the word.

'Chinks,' Seren said. 'Six of 'em, just sitting there, masks over their faces to stop the dust going in their mouths. They don't talk. They don't say anything. They give you a menu to choose from. You point at what you want and they do it. Probably they can't speak English. Don't smile or nothing.'

'They don't ask you where you're going on holiday?'

'They don't ask you anything. Like getting your nails done in a morgue.' She dropped her change on the desk in front of me. It was a good manicure; the beige-pink polish smooth and shiny, the cuticles pushed back even. Joanna didn't ask to see the manicure. Because the manicurists in American Nails were foreign she thought we were home and dry. Even when most of our Christmas business went awry she expected things to get back to normal in the New Year. It was only at the beginning of February when it still hadn't picked up that she started asking around: where did they come from?

Were they illegals? Who was managing the place? Some said they were the wives of the chefs at the new all-you-could-eat Chinese buffet up the valley. Others thought they were illegals, slave labour trafficked by the Triads. Rumours about the manager snowballed. One day he was a twenty-four-year old with a Hummer and a spider web tattoo on his neck. The next day he was nineteen, the Hummer morphed into a Porsche Panamera; the tattoo crept up onto his cheek.

'Nothing new,' my Grancha said, when I told him the story over Sunday lunch at the carvery. 'The Chinese used to be crawling over one another like crabs in a pot here bach. It was the laundries then. They ran the laundries, see.'

It wasn't the first time Joanna had attacked an old customer for switching allegiances. She'd poured a bottle of Bacardi Breezer over Susan Prosser in the NUM club when she'd spotted a receipt from American Nails scrunched up in the bottom of her handbag. It wasn't the first time we'd been on holiday together either. We'd been to Ibiza for a week in March. Basically Joanna took us for company. She didn't have any friends of her own – the woman could start an argument in an empty toilet cubicle. She paid for the flights, the accommodation, our food, drinks, everything, then when we got back she started taking thirty per cent out of our wages to cover it all.

It was early on a Friday evening when we arrived at our apartment in the centre of Benidorm, the day I would have had my interview in Pontypridd. I'd rung the salon manager a few days earlier and told her I wouldn't be able to make it. She refused to cancel the appointment outright. She was impressed with my CV, she said. She'd rearranged it for the following week. We dropped our cases and walked a few blocks east, to a Scottish pub Joanna'd heard about. 'There's a Welsh bar here too,' Seren said as we took our table on the balcony. 'I saw an advert in the reception.'

'Can't go there,' Joanna said, removing her sunglasses and studying the laminated menu. 'I'm banned. Since 1987.' She stared intently at the list of dishes, offering no further explanation. 'Hola!' she shrieked as the waitress approached. 'Scampi and chips times three, and three pints of Buckfast.' She fanned herself with the menu before handing it to the waitress. 'Is that all?' the waitress asked.

'Yep,' Joanna said. 'Maybe some bread and butter.'

I'd wanted to order the Caesar salad. 'I don't like fish,' I said, pins and needles of panic pricking the backs of my legs. 'Yes you do,' Joanna said. 'Anyway, it's scampi. It's not real fish.' The waitress came back with three large glasses of a burgundy-coloured drink. 'Taste it,' Joanna said taking a glass from the tray and passing it to me. It was sweet and viscous, like Calpol. 'Nice,' I said, appeasing her. I thought about ordering a glass of water to go with it but the waitress was already rushing off to another table – the moment passed. Our food came quickly and we unwrapped our cutlery, setting the paper serviettes aside. 'We'll have a quiet one tonight,' Joanna said munching on a chip, 'plenty of time to go mad later; maybe a few drinks in one of the bars on the seafront.' Seren and I exchanged a look. We knew Joanna didn't do quiet.

'Agreed?' Joanna snapped.

'Yes,' Seren whimpered.

Joanna glowered at me.

'Of course,' I said. 'Fine.'

Back at the apartment Joanna poured a large slug of the vodka she'd bought at the airport into a mug from the kitchen cupboard. She emptied her suitcase onto her bed, locating her hair straighteners. 'Chuck us your adaptor,' she said to me. 'I've forgotten mine.' While she was waiting for the plates to heat up she went out onto the balcony where Seren was smoking a cigarette, hand shielding her eyes from the red lozenge sun.

'What's the matter with you?' Joanna asked her. 'Chop chop. We're wasting valuable drinking time hanging around here. Get your glad rags on.' I cringed at the 'glad rags' phrase, the kind of maxim Grancha might have used; but Joanna was forty-one; I suppose it had to be expected. She leant on the balcony railing, her back to the sea view.

'I don't really feel like it, Jo,' Seren mumbled, flicking ash off her cigarette.

'What d'you mean you don't feel like it?' Joanna said. I stepped closer to the patio door, listening for Seren's answer, a can of deodorant tight in my grip. Seren was silent. 'What else are you going to do?' Joanna asked her, her nose wrinkled with disdain.

'Let me lie down for an hour,' Seren said. 'I've got a bit of indigestion. It was that Buckfast stuff; it must have been. I'll be OK later. I'll follow you down.' She stubbed her cigarette out in the ashtray.

'Indigestion?' Joanna said, voice popping with incredulity.

'Bloody sixteen you are, not sixty-one. You're on holiday, Ser.' Seren got up out of her chair and walked limply into the bedroom, ignoring my presence behind the door. She sat back on her bed, her arm crossed over her stomach. Joanna followed her into the bedroom.

'Please, Auntie Jo,' Seren said, before Joanna could speak. 'I'll be OK if you leave me alone for half an hour.'

'PMT you've got, or something,' Joanna said. There was a hot flash of resentment in Seren's eyes, but she didn't pursue the argument. She turned onto her side, drawing her knees up into a foetal position.

'Just me and you then, kid,' Joanna said taking the deodorant out of my hand. She lifted her top and sprayed her armpits, the room clotting with its sweet vanilla scent. We walked down to the seafront and into Acropolis, a small bar cluttered with nautical paraphernalia; fishing nets and rubber sharks. It was lit with a drooping string of Christmas lights tacked to the upper wall. We sat at the bar, Joanna ordering a jug of Sangria for us. She proceeded to pour it, filling her own glass to the top, leaving mine only half full. 'What d'you think's the matter with Madam?' she asked me, the rim of her glass pressed to her face.

I shrugged non-committally. 'She said she had indigestion.'

Joanna screwed her eyes up, as if in disagreement, but said nothing. A group of English boys in their mid-twenties ambled in, their hair cropped close to their skulls, wearing chequered shirts of varying colours and designs. 'Here we go,' Joanna said out of the side of her mouth as the men crowded around us, queuing for drinks. While the one next to her was getting served, Joanna reached around, scratching her neck, strategically elbowing him in the ribs. 'Oh sorry sunshine,' she said turning to face him, and then, eyeing him up and down, 'Well, you're a pretty boy, aren't you? Fancy me bumping into someone as handsome as you.'

It was one in the morning by the time I managed to sneak away. Joanna had made a makeshift dance floor out of the corridor between the gents and the kitchen. She was gyrating to a rap song with her English boy quarry, arching her back, rubbing her haunches against his pelvis, his knobbly workman's hand pressed on the black lycra skirt clung to her hips. I slipped out of the door and began the walk back to the apartment, the clicking sound of grasshoppers lining my route, the bass in the music diluting. All at once I could taste the rusty wine I'd been drinking and the salt blown up from the beach. As I neared our building I heard Joanna calling. Glancing over my shoulder I saw her waddling up the concrete road, her shoes in her hands. I pretended I hadn't. I went into the building hoping that she'd turn back.

The door to the apartment wasn't locked and as I crossed the threshold I felt the atmosphere thicken; the light breeze from outdoors disappeared. The apartment smelled of sweating feet. 'Seren?' Her bed was empty, the covers pulled back. There was a light from under the bathroom door, a thin yellow sliver reflecting on the linoleum in the hall. Seren was crouched in the wheel position at the base of the shower, her legs pulled up, her glossy pedicure reflecting the bare bulb, her naked vagina in full view. 'Seren?' I asked, expecting her to cover herself. She exhaled noisily through her nose. I still couldn't see her face. 'Seren?' I said, stepping closer. I couldn't help staring at her, the way her labia minora resembled a mouth turned onto its side, and then, between the lips, something solid: an orange quarter, peel-side facing out. A baby's head. She was crowning.

'Jesus!' I said, my voice a shock to myself.

'Grr-rrr.' Seren growled and ground her teeth. The baby's head was protruding, moving further and further out of her body, its eyes closed; skin buff-coloured and waxy, like cheap soap. There was a sprinkling of dark fuzz, a Mohican-like band marking the centre of its head. I was kneeling on the bathmat in time to see the body slide clean out. It landed with a smack on the base of the shower tray, its torso the colour of thistle and speckled with blood. The bungee cord landed on its stomach, coiling around itself. I reached out to touch it, then pulled back again before I could. I was too squeamish to touch raw chicken. At home my mother teased me, chasing me around the kitchen with the headless body, its flesh daubed with butter and thyme, ready for the oven.

'Seren?' I said, out of habit now as much as anything else.

'Is it out?' she asked me, her voice tired but full of hope.

'Yeah it's out. I don't know if it's alive.' Seren began to tread backwards, away from the baby, squatting down at the edge of the shower tray. I saw her face for the first time, red and exhausted; broken blood vessels in the whites of her eyes. 'I'll call an ambulance,' I said, the idea a revelation. I knew the emergency number was 112. I'd had to use it in Ibiza when Joanna got into a bar fight. My mobile was like water in my palms. I dropped it twice in a row, the plastic clattering on the bathroom tiles.

'Ambulance please,' I said to the Spanish-speaking voice in the receiver. I could hear the alcohol in my words but I was sober now. The call was over by the time Joanna appeared. She seemed to crash into the room, holding onto the lip of the sink to steady herself. 'Well,' she said, about to launch into some anecdote, when she noticed the tiny body in the shower tray. 'Is that a baby?' she said, matter-of-fact, squinting against the harsh light. 'And where the fuck did you get your toes done? We haven't even got that colour. Cosmic latte. It's still on order.'

'I've called an ambulance,' I said. In no time Joanna had left the room and then returned with a pair of scissors from the kitchen drawer, her fingernails thrust through the plastic handle. She stooped at the base of the shower reaching for the bloodied cord. 'Don't,' Seren said. 'Don't touch me.'

'Don't touch her,' I repeated robotically.

Joanna ignored us, the cord gripped in her hand. With one swift cut she sliced it in half. She picked the baby up, holding it to her midriff, the scissors left on the bathmat. 'Why didn't you tell us, Ser?' she said. 'Why didn't you say anything?' Slowly she began to back away from the shower. She stood in the middle of the bathroom, gently rocking the baby. 'You don't know how lucky you are,' she said, her voice a murmur, an unusual purr. 'What I wouldn't have done for a perfect little baby like this. What did I get, huh? Developmentally disabled, no bloody cure.' She turned the baby in her arms, looking at its face.

'Give him to Seren,' I said.

Joanna looked blankly at Seren, still crouched in the shower tray. 'I had my tubes tied,' she said. 'After Conan. I couldn't risk that again.'

'The ambulance is on its way,' I said. 'Give the baby to Seren, Jo.'

Joanna didn't seem to hear anything I said. Perhaps I wasn't talking at all. 'You don't want a baby, do you?' she asked Seren, as if she was asking her if she wanted a thump. 'Sixteen, you are. Your mother'll do her nut.' She was still rocking the baby, holding its midget hand in her fingers.

'It's Cai's,' Seren said, a squeak from inside the shower cubicle.

We looked at Seren, her head pressed into her hands. 'Who?' Joanna said.

'Cai,' Seren said. 'The manager from American Nails.' And then, a little more forcefully, 'It's my baby, Jo. Give it to me.' She held her arms out for the baby.

Joanna stepped back. 'Come on, Seren,' she said. 'You don't want a baby, do you?' She swung around to face the door and began walking purposefully towards it, her bare feet producing a sharp ripping sound with each step she took.

'Come back, Jo,' I shouted at her. 'Give it to Seren.' I was in the hall following her before I realised I'd moved.

Joanna had slipped out, the front door left open. I stepped out into the corridor. I could hear her, halfway down the stairs.

'Don't leave me,' Seren called, her voice pulling me back.

I went to the patio door, my face squashed against the glass, watching as Joanna staggered toward the beach, the baby still bundled against her chest.

The ambulance took Seren to the clinic. Two policemen drove me to the police station. They sat me down on a wooden chair in an empty room and asked me questions in Spanglish about Joanna and her whereabouts. 'She went to the beach,' I told them, repeating myself until all I could hear was my blood beating against the sides of my skull, my tongue so dry I couldn't shape it around words. Later they locked me alone in a cell, a thin scratchy blanket, like a potato sack, in my hand. I twisted around on the mattress, trying to get comfortable, feeling every metal spring. I fell into a hypnotic doze, encountering short bursts of dream in one part of my brain, a cold, hazy reality in the other. At one point I was sure I heard Joanna's voice echoing in the corridor outside. 'Mental impairments,' she was shrieking, over and over again. 'Mental impairments, American Nails. Mental impairments, American Nails.'

When I woke a policeman and a plain-clothed woman with ginger hair were standing in the doorway to the cell. I could see a ration of daylight through the air vent underneath the sink. 'Kayla?' the woman said. 'I'm a representative from the British Embassy.' She had a thick

Birmingham accent and freckles on her cleavage. 'I've come to help you, alright?' She drove me to our apartment in the town centre and walked me into the building. The front door was sealed with yellow policia tape. I stopped, gawking at it. 'It's OK,' she said. 'We're just going to collect your things. We've got permission.' She took the key from my hand and opened the door, peeling the tape and ducking underneath it. The sweating feet odour had gone, replaced with aloe vera; the potted cacti and flora from the balcony. 'Which suitcase is yours?' Together we threw my possessions into my pink wheelie suitcase, my flip-flops, my underwear, my clunky adaptor plug. Joanna's hair straighteners were still on the bed, opened to a V shape.

'Some of my toiletries are in the bathroom,' I said, hoping the woman would fetch them for me. I didn't want to see the blood stains, or the scissors on the bathmat. 'Go on then, bab,' she said with a thin smile. 'You'll have to go. I won't know what belongs to you, what belongs to Seren.' She pronounced Seren with an extra E, serene. She didn't mention Jo. The shower was hidden behind a white plastic sheet, another strip of police tape securing it. I took my can of deodorant and bottle of CK One from the shelf above the sink and went back to the common room area.

'Are you ready to go to the airport?' the woman asked. 'There's a flight to Gatwick leaving in three and a half hours.' I nodded. 'And you're sure you have funds to pay for it?' I had three hundred pounds of credit left on the card I'd used for my GNVQ course.

My mother was waiting at the terminal building in

London. She hugged me too tightly. We didn't speak until we arrived at Leigh Delamere Services two hours later. 'Seren's still at the clinic,' she said while we waited in the queue at the till. 'Retained placenta. She didn't pass the afterbirth. But they'll see to that. She'll be alright. Joanna they've arrested for infanticide.'

'Infanticide?' I asked, opening my purse and realising I only had Euros.

'Murder,' she said, 'of a baby. I knew something wasn't right about that woman. I knew it was only a matter of time.'

I zipped my purse closed. 'I don't think she killed the baby,' I said.

'Shh,' my mother said. We were getting closer to the cashier. Speaking without moving her lips she said, 'you'll get a chance to tell your side of the story. They'll call you back to Benidorm for the trial, worst luck.' She paid for our things and we sat down in the food court. I peeled the cellophane back on my pre-prepared sandwich. My mother reached across the table, patting at my wrist.

'I'm not ill,' I said. My stomach was rumbling. I stuffed the corner of my sandwich into my mouth, the mayonnaise cool and slick on my tongue. I retched suddenly, dropping the sandwich. The chunk I'd bitten off I spat into my paper napkin. Roast chicken. I couldn't get that picture of Seren out of my mind's eye: her body flipped backward on the shower tray, red, raw and opened; the baby between her feet. Seren's creamy, milk-coloured toenails. 'But I'm not hungry,' I said, pushing the sandwich and its packaging away. 'You need to build yourself up nice and strong,' my mother said. 'You've got that interview in Pontypridd in a few days. It's a trauma you've been through; you don't know it yet.'

But I did. I didn't want to go anywhere near a nail salon again.

Desire Lines

The house on Hilgard Avenue wears its Kappa Kappa Gamma credentials on its sleeve; two-foot Greek letters embossed above the front door, the Martha Stewart-style floral drapes drawn. I check the address on the postcard for the last time, though it's stamped on my brain like my own SSN. I settle down on the acid-green lawn to finish the reefer I started back in Missouri, 'Misery' as Jess'd call it. I should have known she'd end up in a place like this: utopian cookie-cutter nightmare. I've been travelling fourteen hours straight. I watched the LA sunrise peek through buttermilk clouds at the perimeter of the city, the bus coasting through jagged oilfields, pump jacks like oversize praying mantes lapping hungrily at their spoils. After an hour the sun is out in full, the cloud dispersed. I'm craving baby back ribs and blueberry cake donut when I hear movement, not from the house but a rowdy bunch of students heading slowly up the drive. I sit on my guitar case so they can't steal it from me too easily. The acoustic is all I have left. I had to pawn the Billy Morrison to buy the bus ticket.

A sycamore trunk is blocking my view of them, but then, as they emerge, I see there are only three people, a leggy brunette tottering on patent stilettos, and a couple. The girl is a blonde in a blue taffeta dress, hanging off the man's arm. I sense it's Jessica the moment I clap eyes on her though she looks different: florid pink lipstick staining her mouth; the prissy, navy gown at least a decade too old for her. They pull away from one another, the jock in a dinner suit, rushing towards me. 'What is your business here, buddy?' he says.

'Jessica?' I mouth it rather than say it, my voice lost amid the furore.

Jess hangs back on the sidewalk, squinting in my direction. The brunette takes her arm, as if in fear.

'Listen man,' the jock says. He's standing above me, muscled shins a couple of centimetres away from my face. 'This house is Kappa, the sisters' house. You've got no business here now, have you?' His breath smells like mint Lifesavers and somehow I know he's kissed her.

'Jessica?' I say. 'Jessica Rabbit? You remember me?'

She's silent for a long time, long enough for me to suspect she's going to pretend she's never met me, her face a soup of dread and embarrassment, the sun kissing the fine splatter of freckles on the bridge of her nose. I go for the proof, the postcard in my pocket. 'Ryan,' she says finally, resignedly. 'What are you doing here?' She asks the question as if my being there is impossible, an illusion.

'Greyhound,' I tell her shrugging.

'You know this stoner, Jessie?' the jock asks her.

Stoner? Christ on a fucking paddle boat. 'Stoner? You think you're auditioning for Grease III or something, dipshit? Get out of my face, man. Let me talk to my girl.' I'm not scared and I demonstrate this by refusing to stand up and face him. He looks to Jess for instructions. She nods sulkily. 'I'm less than two minutes away,' he warns me. 'At the Delta Phi, a block across.' To Jess he says, 'Call me later, or earlier if you get any trouble.'

Of course it wasn't like this when we met last summer. If anything, it was the reverse. My band, my old band, had a gig at The Hurricane on Broadway in Kansas City. We were getting to the middle of our set when she appeared, sprite-like, out of nowhere, jumping on a kid in the moshpit, all hot pants and fishnet pantyhose. She blew me off in the back of the van, Gerard and Scott rapping on the door trying to load their gear. I fucked her quickly. She said she wanted it that way. Then she wrote her number across the back of my hand in black Sharpie. I guess it was a cliché, looking back, but hell, it worked for me. I couldn't quite scrub the digits off my skin, not with soap, not with the specialist cleaner from my brother's garage. I called her a couple of days later and we met at the Bake Shop on Main Street. She cut a childish figure, sitting on a high stool swinging her legs, a banana milkshake on the table in front of her. There was no trace of the green beer bottle that'd been glued in her fist the other night, the animal lust gone from her eyes.

She wasn't the kind of girl I usually attracted. In high school there'd been Alison, a 196 lb compulsive liar, obsessed with English heavy metal bands from the 70s, who swore blind she'd once 'time-travelled' back to the London gin epidemic. And then, Brandy, a bisexual Candidate Master Chess player who attacked me with one of her brother's golf irons. I thought I'd lucked out when I met Renée, the older woman, who'd pick me up in her 1978 Pontiac and drive us into the Mark Twain National Forest to teach me flawless cunnilingus. Turned out she was married, to the colonel at the Boone County Sheriff's Department. Jess seemed kind of normal, like the girlfriends the other guys had.

'I have to tell you something,' she said. She slurped the last of the milkshake through the heart-shaped drinking straw. 'I'm having a tough time of it at the moment. My parents are getting divorced and I've been acting sort of crazy. Not my usual self. I was a little drunk and I made a big mistake.' She wiped her mouth with her paper napkin. 'You do understand?' She scrunched the napkin into a ball, indicating the end of our conversation. But three days after that she called me back. 'I have to tell you something,' she said, a new exigency to her voice.

'Again?' I said.

'Yes again, Ryan. I'm pregnant.'

I met her the third time at the abortion clinic, which turned out to be two blocks away from my house, a nondescript, white stucco box. I guess I always thought it was some kind of Mormon Church. She was wearing a pair of khaki clam diggers, tear tracks ploughing through thick, beige make-up. 'Thanks for coming,' she yelped at me between sobs, which, you have to admit, is kind of ironic. She flashed an appreciative smile at me as we sat down in the waiting room. It was then that I fell in love with her, the vulnerability, the freckles; a big man's longing for small women. 'Listen,' I said taking her hand. 'You don't have to do this. It isn't ideal. Well, we don't even know each other. But so what?' I stole a glance at her belly. 'Maybe it's an augury, the start of something. You know?'

'An augury?' She whipped her hand back, crossing her arms over her waist. 'Biology more like,' she said out the side of her mouth. 'You promised me you wouldn't do this,' she added, her voice turned low, a tormented repine. 'I told you. It's my body. It's none of your business. Don't be a jerk.'

'Except it sort of is my business,' I said. I guess I couldn't help myself. Who knew that I, Ryan Shaughnessy, was capable of making a baby? That my spermatozoon was the healthy kind, not the type you saw filmed under microscopes in biology lessons; double-tailed and slow as molasses? On cue the clerk called me over to the desk to pay. I pulled Gerard's father's leather-bound checkbook out of my jeans pocket and forged a bill for $300. Turned out later it bounced, but hell, they couldn't pump the foetus back in. 'It's for the best,' she said when I got back to the seat. 'I'm not ready to have a kid, not with you, not with anyone. I'm going to UCLA next year, the school of dentistry; I'm going to be an orthodontist.'

'There's a great school of dentistry at Mizzou,' I told her, and there was, though I'm not sure how I knew that.

'Yeah,' she said, dismissively. 'But I want to live in LA, the sunshine, the glamour. And anyway, I'll have kids when I'm married.' Before I could think up a retort she added, 'I'll make sure I marry right, not somebody like my Daddy who'll fuck his secretary the first chance he gets.'

'We could get married,' I told her. 'I don't have a secretary. I don't even have a job.'

'Exactly,' she said. 'You don't even have a job.' She turned away, staring obstinately at an advert for contraception on the clinic wall.

I guess she'd gone and gotten herself caught up in the distorted notion that life should and always would be fair, not something I ever suffered from. When your father's in prison and your mother's half brain dead, confined to an electric-powered wheelchair, you expect there's some curveballs coming for you too. Still, I liked that she was innocent, and kind of naive, and I made it my mission in life to keep her that way. That'd be a good, honourable achievement I reckoned, and besides, my brother always said I was the type to wander where whimsy led.

Now the jock heads down a clearing between the lupines, checking me intermittently over his shoulder. The brunette goes into the house, watching us through a gap in the floral drapes. 'I didn't think you'd come all this way,' Jess says grasping sheepishly at her silk skirt. 'I can see that,' I say. I move along the neck of the guitar, offering her a seat next to me on the case, which she declines. 'You remember what you wrote on this postcard you sent me?' I ask her. I offer her the postcard with its vintage sepia photograph of the Miracle Mile. She waves it away impatiently, lips pursed angrily.

'What?' she barks. I finger the crease forked through the Mullen & Bluett building, and turn it over, pointing out her handwriting. 'Wish you were here.'

'For God's sake, Ryan. It's just a phrase, an old chestnut. You weren't meant to take it so literally.' She reaches for the bobby pin holding her bangs out of her face, releasing it with a sigh. 'You've chosen a really bad time. I'm busy studying for my end of year practicals. They're starting next week.'

'Yeah, you sure look busy Jess.'

'Well I am! And you know you can't stay here, right? This is a sorority house. No men allowed.'

'So now what?' I ask her. She pokes at her thumbnail with the edge of the pin, breathing through her nose. 'I'll call you,' she says. 'After my exams. If you're still here maybe we could do lunch?' She turns, gazing dutifully at the house. 'If my group leader sees you out here my ass'll be on the line. It's all I've ever wanted, to live in a sorority house. You know how hard I had to work at rush week to get in here? Don't ruin this for me, Ryan. Please.'

After two long nights under a bleacher in De Longpre Park, I find a cheap, long stay motel off the Ventura Freeway in North Hollywood, the exterior walls painted a noisy canary yellow. The proprietor, a fat, shark-eyed man with lanky, comb-over hair says I can use my driver licence as a deposit and pay my first rent in a week's time. I get a room on the top floor overlooking the macadam parking lot, the sweat-stained pillow alive with head lice. Overnight I notice the place is occupied almost exclusively by middle-aged dipsomaniacs, bloated and toothless. They come and go, staggering dangerously around the edge of the empty pool, bottles of mescal concealed in paper bags. A pensioner in a threadbare plaid robe stays out all night playing chess with himself, shrieking like a coyote every time it's his move.

Mid-morning I take my guitar to the Wholefoods Market catty-corner, setting up on the sidewalk at the approach. I busk for eight hours straight, Beatles and REO Speedwagon numbers, stopping only to munch on a couple of peanut butter Graham crackers. At six there're a few coins in the takeaway carton next to me, including two half dollars. I'm about ready to pack up when a beat-up F150 pick-up crawls into the lot. The driver's a dwarf with a shocking spray of blue-black hair, silver hoop earrings too big for her frame. She parks up near the back of the lot and turns her engine off. I wait for her to get out and head into the store. I guess I've never seen a real-life dwarf before. But she stays sitting in the driver's seat, smoking a menthol cigarette. Gradually other pick-ups and cars arrive, pulling up next to her, yakking to her through their windows before turning and leaving a couple of minutes later. A bunch of teenagers arrive on foot and march along the dirt-track desire-lines carved in the grass verges, their Converse sneakers caked with dried mud. They form a line at the door of the pick-up, flashes of tin foil exchanging hands. Almost instinctively I start strumming 'Free Fallin'', so as not to appear conspicuous. It's the first song I learned, the only riff I don't need to concentrate on. Before the song is finished the teenagers have gone. The dwarf lady's heading for the exit, slowing up as she sidles alongside me. She crumples a $10 note in her hand, pitching it into my carton. 'Thank you, Ms,' I say, unable to conceal my gratitude.

'You know "Cherry, Cherry" by Neil Diamond?' she says, her voice a sunny clang, like a dinner triangle. She has a turn in her left eye, and I try not to focus on it. 'That's my song! My name is Cherry.'

'I could learn it I guess,' I tell her. She throws me a jaunty wink. Without thinking about it I return it in kind.

A week turns into two; two into three. There is no phone call from Jess, only a couple of irate answer phone messages from my brother in Kansas City demanding I get back and do my share of the housework. I manage to pay some money towards my room with Gerard's father's checkbook. It'll probably bounce, if it hasn't already, so I spend my time sneaking out the fire exit at the motel, avoiding the proprietor, trampling over a few fences to go busking in the Riverside Drive parking lot. Every evening, Cherry, the indigo-haired dwarf, rolls up in her red pick-up, leaving again half an hour later. Usually, but not always, she hurls a $10 note my way along with that same, bold signature wink. It's the only recurring contact I have with another human being and I come to anticipate our flirtation, little flames of fervour licking up inside of me for hours beforehand. On a particularly humid night, towards the end of the month, her pink T-shirt clinging to disproportionate breasts, she blows me a cheeky kiss. 'How ya doin', guitar boy?' she asks me.

'What are you hawking over there?' comes my clumsy reply. I guess I'm jonesing for a toke. It's been a while.

'Crack and crystal meth,' she says, brazen. 'A girl's gotta make a living somehow.' She eyes me over the smoke from her cigarette. The concentration in her face collapses into a crooked smile, loosening a horde of silverfish inside me. 'You learned my song yet?' she says.

I shake my head. 'I tried, but-' my words trail off sadly. A few days ago I stole a Neil Diamond tab book from a record store on Moorpark Street but it didn't have the song and I've never heard it played.

'Don't matter,' she says. 'I'll take you on a date this weekend if you want. Ya know Santa Monica beach ain't too far away?' I've been in LA for three weeks and I've yet to see the Capitol Records Building or the Whiskey on Sunset Strip. Seamlessly my life has slid into an inescapable hand-to-mouth regime. I'm overjoyed at the prospect of a trip to the beach. 'Sure,' I say playing along with her.

Early on Saturday morning she picks me up at the approach to the Wholefoods Market, her eyes plastered with sticky blue eye-shadow, the sun reflecting in the grains of glitter caked on her lids. 'You ain't got your guitar?' she says frowning at me as I climb into the passenger seat of the pick-up.

'No.' I've hidden it in the Johnsongrass half a mile from the motel. I figure it's safer there than in my own room. 'Why?' I notice my hands are trembling slightly, as though my body's convinced itself that this is a regular, bone fide date. Whatever she wants from me, I'm sure it's not a boyfriend. I guess I have a vague hope that she'll offer me some work.

'No reason,' she says quickly adjusting her raised driving seat. 'Never seen ya without it's all.' Her brake and gas pedals are hand controls next to the wheel, the cab floor littered with layers of cigarette packets and junk food cartons. 'You recognise me?' she asks glancing in my direction when we're a couple of miles along the Freeway.

'Should I?' I ask, worried. Maybe she's one of them crazies you see on America's Most Wanted, some hitwoman hired by the Delta Phi jock.

'Hell yeah! I'm a star, y'know. A real Hollywood actress.'

'Yeah?' I ask sceptically. 'What've you been in?'

'A Kathy Bates movie, an episode of Seinfeld, a couple of TV movies,' she pauses a moment and adds, 'the other stuff too. Porn.' She gestures at the back seat; a stack of video tapes in a thin plastic grocery bag. There's a picture of her on the one at the top, wearing lurid green Lycra lingerie, her thighs white and puffy like a newborn baby's. The movie's called Itty Bitty Gangbang. 'I thought we might watch a couple later,' she says. 'If it goes well, y'know?'

I stifle a flustered cough. 'Sure, I'll try anything twice,' I say, my voice high and oddly effeminate, my eyes threatening to water. Her candour is a comfort after Jess's running hot and cold, but the thought of sex with a dwarf is unnerving. What position would we need to employ? What if I hurt her? She surveys me sideways with her crossed eye. I can't be sure if she's just checking the passenger side mirror. 'I'm joking, dumb-ass,' she says. 'I ain't no goddamned slut. I do the movies, sure.

Fuck on a first date? Me? Never.' I guess I'm pleased about that but I don't want to risk offending her by admitting it.

'You should be living up in the hills, all those movies you've done,' I tell her. 'Why would you want to peddle crack in North Hollywood?'

'The movies don't pay as much as ya think,' she says. 'Not for someone like me. ''Sides, I like to keep my options open. I like to be self-sufficient.'

'Oh, you're that alright,' I say.

'Have to be,' she says. 'Ya know I'm Armenian? My folks live in Little Armenia over in East Hollywood, and Armenians have an aversion to little people, a superstition.' She affects a weak European accent. '"Stand away from the dwarfs because it's God who hit them on the head." I've been taking care of myself since I turned twelve years old. Weren't nobody else gonna to do it for me. When I was a kid my older brothers used to prop me on top of the closet, leave me up there for hours on end and make me catch popcorn in my mouth.'

'Bummer,' is all I can muster.

We park in a disabled space overlooking the pier, the famous Santa Monica Ferris wheel high in the blue sky above us. Out of the truck she averages four foot, her head level with my ribcage. I see for the first time that she walks with a severe limp, her left knee stiff and swollen. She swings her foot in a half circle before planting it on the ground: kLOMPa-whap-SHLINK, kLOMPa-whap-SHLINK, but she does it quickly, the crowds on the boardwalk parting to let us through, a blur of faceless colour as we march over the wooden slats.

We reach the park gates in a minute flat. Then it takes the attendant at the rollercoaster ten minutes to strap Cherry into a disabled carriage at the front. I sit directly behind her, perusing the crowds as we take our long chugging journey to the summit. It's while I'm there, at the top, waiting for the downhill stage to begin, that I notice Jessica Rabbit stood on the pier below. She's with the jock and the brunette, and a couple of other people, wearing a black-and-white-print party dress, clutch purse in her hand. I've been staring at her for a few seconds when she turns and looks straight up at me, as if she'd been able to feel my eyes on her body, her blonde hair whipping around in the wind. My first instinct is to wave, but I stop myself, sitting on my hands. I turn my gaze on the vast turquoise ocean. The last thing I'm going to do is start fantasising Jessica out of thin air. This date is strange enough all on its own.

'Awesome!' Cherry yells as the attendant releases her from her carriage. She presses on her breasts, making sure they haven't escaped her skimpy vest top. Something about this gesture seems to bring out the protector in me. I put my arm around her, guiding her as she alights from the ride.

'Stay right here so I don't lose you,' she says, wagging her finger as we step down onto the boardwalk. She begins to clomp away, shouting back at me over her shoulder. 'I'm gonna get us some hush pups from Bubba Gumps.' She points at a little restaurant a little further along the pier. 'Best shrimp ya'll ever taste, boy.' I try to follow her but a little kid blocks my path with his remote control Porsche, sending it in a circular track around my feet, rooting me to the spot. I should pay for the food, I think, and I riffle through my pants pocket while I wait for the kid to get lost, Cherry melding into the blurry, anonymous crowd.

'You've got a job?' Jess is stood facing me, her clutch purse at her hip. With her other hand she shades her eyes from the sun, her arm sleek and tan. I let go of the dimes in my pocket, my mouth going dry. 'A job?' I say repeating half of her sentence.

'You've got a job taking care of the handicapped?' she says. It's less of a question, more of a statement, her eyes expectant. She seems to nod, imploring me to mimic her. The gold bracelet on her wrist slides down her forearm, coming to rest in front of her perfect, pert cleavage.

'Yeah, kinda,' I say. I guess I can't help myself.

'Wow, Ryan. That's so sweet. I knew you had it in you to do something worthwhile. Really worthwhile.' She toys briefly with a button on my shirt, sending electric currents surging along my aorta. 'I'm here with a few friends,' she says. 'Celebrating. I passed my first year.' I glance over my shoulder, worried Cherry's on her way back. She isn't. 'Yeah?' I say to Jess. 'Good for you.'

The Delta Phi jock is a couple of metres away, watching us greedily. He puts his fingers to his mouth, whistling. 'Your master calls,' I tell Jess. She rolls her eyes. 'So you're sticking around for a while?' she asks me. 'LA's great, isn't it?'

'Sure.' I expect her to leave now but she doesn't. She looks into my eyes, waiting for more. There's nothing to say and she's yet to apologise for not calling. I drop eye contact, feigning interest in the boardwalk. The rush of the ocean underneath it makes me feel a little slap-happy. 'I'm staying at the Rest Haven motel off the Ventura Freeway,' I say, looking up. I'm not sure why. Why do we tell anybody anything? The jock whistles a second time.

'Really?' Jess says to me, ignoring him. 'Maybe I'll drop by some time. I'm proud of you, Ryan. You should know that.' She locks her arms around my neck and pecks my cheek, her anti-perspirant lemon-scented. Her smile reminds me of our morning in the abortion clinic. My heart misses a beat as she turns to walk away. I step backward, numb with a new disappointment, feeling something buckle under my foot. I realise it's the kid's remote control Porsche, the wing snapped off, the glass shattered.

'Asshole!' the kid sneers up at me, his angelic ash-blond hair catching sunrays. It's then that Cherry reappears, paper cartons of deep-fried shrimp in either hand. 'You're an asshole,' she tells the kid as she kicks the remainder of his remote control car over the edge of the pier.

Later that night I'm supine on the iron bed at the motel, drunk, and stoned off a big bag of skunk Cherry produced on the drive back to North Hollywood, my brain turned to cotton. She's sitting on me, reverse cowgirl style, blue-black curls brushing against her shoulder blades. All I can feel are her lumpy buttocks grinding against the tops of my thighs. I guess she doesn't have the height to get the purchase right. Also I'm surprised I've managed to get any kind of erection;

I can hardly see straight. It's dark save for the ghost light of the television, a Creedence Clearwater Revival CD blaring out of Cherry's battery-operated ghetto blaster to suppress the squawking from the lone chess player outside, the neck of the acoustic propped next to the bed, hammering against the bedside cabinet.

The constant juddering of the bed pulls Jess's postcard from out of its hiding place under the lice-infested pillow. I'm hiding it again, in the hollow of the guitar when I see a pair of black kitten heels propped in the doorway. Jess is stood in them, watching, a champagne bottle in her hand. I blink a few times, resisting the hallucination, but it doesn't go away. 'Jessica?' I mouth the word, squinting at her uncertainly. Without any warning she flies across the room, knocking Cherry off the bed like a bull tripping a matador. Cherry lands on the floor. Jessica stoops over her body, yelling. 'What the hell are you doing to him? The first job he's had in his life. You're going to screw it all up.'

Cherry drives her fist upwards, hitting Jessica in the temple. The champagne bottle goes rolling, a kitten heel flying into the closet door. Cherry struggles onto her feet.

'Cool it, the both of you,' I say, covering myself with the sheet.

'Cool it?' Cherry says, incredulous. 'Nobody lays their stinkin' hands on me. Nobody tells me to cool it.' She takes hold of Jessica's limp wrists, dragging her to the hallway, Jess's dress collecting dust bunnies as she goes. Cherry's bare feet stomp on the floorboards with the whole weight of her little body: kLOMPa-whap-SHLINK, kLOMPa-whap-SHLINK. 'Who is your mother, girlfriend?'

she hollers at Jess, letting go of one of her wrists, stopping to scratch at her own mound of dark pubic hair. 'Seems she forgot to teach you any manners, lady,' she says taking Jess's wrist up again. 'She forgot to teach you to knock.'

I'm too weak and dizzy to raise myself off the mattress. I watch through the crack in the door as Cherry deposits Jess's flaccid body at the top of the stairwell. 'Find your way back down them steps there, girlfriend,' she says leaving her and heading back to the bedroom. 'You know that crackhead?' she asks me, stood naked and akimbo in the doorway.

I shake my head. I guess I can't help myself.

'This place of yours ain't nothing but weirdos,' she says. 'Filthy too.' She goes for her pubic hair again, scraping mercilessly at herself. 'I think I caught crabs since I been here.' She sees the champagne bottle buttressed against the base board. 'Least we can toast our first date,' she says picking it up.

'Sure,' I murmur.

She leaps onto the edge of the bed, her legs dangling as she fidgets with the mesh top of the glass bottle. 'You sure you don't know her?' she asks me, gesturing with a flick of her head at the doorway, and Jess, beyond it. 'I mean what was she goin' on about, first job you ever had?'

'Search me,' I shrug. 'Never seen her before in my life.'

'Weirdo,' Cherry says under her breath, and then: 'We've gotta get you outta this motel, boy. My place ain't much but it's a royal palace compared to this. You can move in with me tomorrow.' She applies a little pressure to the champagne cork, removing it deftly without spilling a drop.

The Milstein Kosher Liquorice Co.

'There's Ellis Island right there,' Abe squawked, practically jumping up and down on the spot. 'Look bubbeleh! We made it!'

Sasha studied the building, eyes tearful in the wind. The building was smaller than she'd imagined, a gothic terracotta structure, gingerbread turrets on its nearside. She felt the swelling in her ankles as she staggered down the gangplank, the sudden daylight a concussion. She'd only counted three full days. Something was wrong. They couldn't be in America yet. 'Where's the Statue of Liberty?' she asked. She wanted to see the Statue of Liberty. Maybe then she could believe it.

'That's somewhere else,' Abe said waving into the distance. 'On a different island.' Sasha squinted against the stinging cold, searching for it. But there was no other island, only the murky, choppy water. A deckhand shouted down at them in a language they didn't understand, gesturing at them to move along with the other passengers. Chaotic clusters of people were heading in the opposite direction, away from the Ellis Island immigration station. The majority of them were Christians, the people Abe and Sasha had come here to avoid. A man in a heavy, navy apron counted heads as the crowds pushed through a metal barrier. There was no health inspection, no chalk disc inscribed on their lapels as Abe's cousins had sworn there would be. 'You are sure this is America?' Sasha asked her husband, the salt air hitting the back of her throat.

'Sure I am sure,' Abe said happily.

She saw one of the Lithuanian-speaking crew members fighting through the crowd, heading back towards the ship. 'This is New York?' she asked him.

'New York,' he nodded, smiling to himself when he'd passed.

Levi and Isaac had promised to meet the couple on the dockside but after an hour Abe and Sasha were still waiting, their trunk on the pavement at their feet. 'Maybe they're in a tavern nearby,' Abe said eventually, turning to face the city. He began to schlep the trunk across the street, the weight of it twisting his back. 'Drinking?' Sasha muttered as she traipsed after him. 'That would be just like your family, wouldn't it?' Abe's cousins had always been a bad influence, intent on taking Abe to the inn in the centre of Rietavas to drink schnapps and argue politics. Night after night he'd returned home drunk and belligerent. He wasn't an aggressive man – just the opposite; far too easily led. He hadn't touched a drop of hooch since his cousins had left for America a year earlier. Sasha wasn't overjoyed at the prospect of Abe meeting up with them again. 'Booze-fuelled counterfeiters,' she said, repeating an aspersion she'd heard on the streets of the old town.

Abe continued walking regardless, unable to hear his wife's sly protests. The noise in the city was riotous: a brew of drums and bells and piano, howls from seafarers, caterwauls from women, the constant wavering swish of the water. A man wheeled a barrel organ towards them, a peculiar furry animal on his shoulder. 'Shalom,' Abe said in greeting, hoping the man was Jewish but the man answered, 'Hello,' in English and then continued on his way. The couple stood on tiptoes glowering through the dirty windows of cafés and bars. They saw a group of Chinamen gambling with coloured seashells, their laughter turning their eyes to fine black perforations in sturdy yellow skin. They saw all kinds of people, but no Jews, and definitely no Levi or Isaac Milstein. 'Face it, Abe,' Sasha said when she was too tired to walk any further. 'Your cousins are liars. We're wasting our time going round and round in circles.' She looked at the arsenic-grey sky, avoiding eye contact with her husband. She rubbed at her extended belly. 'I need to lie down now, Abe. I need to rest.'

Soon the couple were on the doorstep of a boarding house, a bewildered-looking landlady staring at them. Sasha mimed her intention, her hands pressed together, set at the side of her head. Abe offered the woman some of the American money his cousins had sent him. The woman looked disappointed but she took it and showed them to a room at the very top of the narrow row house.

Sasha tested the bed while Abe drew a letter from the pocket of his shirt. He brought the onionskin page up close to his face, reading aloud his cousins' instructions for entering America. 'At the island an inspector will ask you questions-'

'Nobody asked us any questions,' Sasha said. She was curled in a foetal position, the rough woollen blanket pulled up to her chin.

'But they wouldn't just desert us like this,' Abe said, squinting again at the page. 'They know we cannot afford guesthouses.'

Sasha shrugged. 'How can you know that? Men as useless as the product they deal in? Men with flavoured liquorice for brains?' She stopped talking when the landlady arrived with a tray of tea and sat up, watching her set the drinks on the ottoman at the bottom of the bed. The landlady seemed to sense the tension in the room, curtsying briskly before retreating.

'Wartn,' Abe called to the landlady. 'Wait! Broikline Brick,' he said, attempting to quote from the letter in English. 'What is the way to the Broikline Brid?'

'The Brooklyn Bridge?' the woman said. 'You're looking for the Brooklyn Bridge?' She leant against the doorjamb looking from Sasha to Abe and back again, her fingers smoothing the seam of her cardigan. 'This is Cardiff,' she said. 'Wales. There's no Brooklyn Bridge in this city.'

'No Broikline Brick?' Abe asked, his voice high with desperation.

Sasha snorted at her husband's incompetence.

'You're in Wales, my love,' the woman said. 'Great

Britain.' She straightened herself, stepping backwards onto the landing. 'Enjoy your refreshments,' she said as she turned, beginning down the staircase.

Anger launched Sasha off the bed, dropping her upright, an inch away from Abe. She plucked the letter from his hand and tore it, throwing the pieces unceremoniously into his face. Abe remained standing, his eyes closed, the notepaper confetti raining over his shoulders like Lithuanian snow. 'Is that all you can do?' she challenged him. 'Stand there like a cow, your mouth in your collar? You dumb idiot! I told you this wasn't America. We had only been on the ship for two nights.' She held two fingers in the air. 'How could it be America? But whoever listens to me? A stupid girl? Ach, I am the only one with any sense.' She threw her weight down on the mattress a little too dramatically, hurting herself. 'You can sleep on the floor,' she ordered.

Abe sat down on the ottoman, a scrap of paper still stuck to his earlobe. He held his head in his hands. 'A trickster,' he sighed. 'A low down dirty conman. A hoax, the whole crew in on it.'

Sasha watched him narrow-eyed. 'They saw you coming,' she hissed at him. 'So eager to impress your father-in-law, you thought nothing of your wife!'

Abe began to sob, his shoulders jerking. In the half-light Sasha saw one of his tears land on the wooden tea tray, large enough to bounce once before dispersing. A heartache mushroomed out of her rage. 'Oh, Abe,' she said, her voice low with shame. She approached him slowly, moving the tea tray to the floor. 'I thought I was doing the right thing by you,' he said as she sat down beside him gingerly, his olive-green eyes turned lightless.

Sasha stroked his arm. 'I know you did bubbeleh, I know.' This is how the cogs of Abe and Sasha's marriage turned. Sasha pecked at Abe, hoping to strike a well of machismo but there was only naivety, a boyish innocence that begged to be nurtured. 'Who, but us, could buy a ticket to America and end up a hundred miles out of London?' she asked with a fragile, nervous laugh. 'Maybe we could look on it as an adventure,' she said, knowing as she spoke that her husband was not the adventurous type. He knew how to dream. If dreaming was a sport he'd have ten medals. But adventures were something else.

It had been an inauspicious start to the year in their hometown on the Jūra River. On the 2nd of January 1903, a vagrant had found the body of a thirteen-year-old Rietavas girl, stabbed and debased in a field to the north. The killer had tried to take her head off with one clean blow, the daisies around her body stained crimson. The girl was Christian, last seen alive accompanying her grandparents to the liturgy, and so it was obvious, to the tattlers in the market at least, that Jews were responsible for the death; that they wanted her blood to thicken their Kiddush wine. There was already trouble stirring across the border in Russia. By late January groups of Christians stood in the street throwing eggs at Jewish passers-by. 'It is an old story,' Sasha's father said at the Sabbath table. 'Soon they will start with the looting. I am old enough to know just how it will go. You have family in America already, nu?' he asked Abe.

'Yes sir,' Abe said. 'My cousins Levi and Isaac run a

very profitable business from a warehouse at the base of the Brooklyn Bridge; the Milstein Kosher Liquorice Co.' Sasha's father chuckled. Sasha had thought that he was mocking Abe. Who ever had heard of kosher liquorice? But she knew now the source of her father's pleasure; planting so easily the seed of America in his son-in-law's tiny mind. 'In the new world the Jews are free from religious persecution, you know?' he said. 'Whatever happens here, your cousins will be safe.'

Dangerously loyal, and hungry for the mealiest scrap of acclaim, Abe went to the Rietavas Bank on Sunday morning, withdrawing all the money he'd saved working at the armchair factory. For three years the money had sat unworried, earmarked for one of the new Izba houses being built on the other side of the river. He met with a businessman at the port in Klaipėda, procuring two passages to America, paying a little extra for third class over steerage so that Sasha would be comfortable on the long Atlantic crossing. There was no printed ticket, just a small rusted washer for a receipt. Had she known what her husband was planning Sasha would have tried to intervene. Instead her fate was handed to her, sealed, over the Seder plate on the first day of Pesach. Her mother brought the hand-washing bowl to the table for the sixth part of the Haggadah. Abe, eager to assist, slid his wine along the table, making space for the bowl. As usual he moved too quickly, knocking the wine against the horseradish crock. It spilled over the best linen tablecloth.

'Klutz,' Sasha reprimanded him under her breath.

Her father coughed, catching his daughter's eye. 'Do

not be so quick to chastise your husband,' he said. 'The beauty of a woman is in her silence. Besides, he is a benevolent man-' He looked to Abe to take the conversation up.

'We are going to America, Sasha,' Abe said. 'We are going to America to start our lives afresh! Your husband a vendor at the highly successful Milstein Kosher Liquorice Co., your unborn son a stranger to anti-Semitism.' He raised his glass. 'Mazel Tov!'

Sasha's mother was leaning over the table, dabbing at the cloth with white vinegar. She paused sharply, glancing sceptically at her son-in-law. 'What about me?' Sasha said. 'What about your wife? I'm pregnant. A pregnant woman-' her words trailed off, unnecessary; to her mind even a man should understand that a woman, pregnant for the first time, would like to be close to her own mother. 'Do you not understand?' her father asked. 'In America your child will flourish. Because of you our descendants will survive.'

Before the end of Pesach Sasha was boarding *The Empress of Eros*, expecting to disembark in New York City. At least the winters there would not be so bitter, she thought.

The next morning found Abe and Sasha face to face, breathing the same sour Great British air. Sasha turned on her back, staring at the ceiling. The rigging of a ship creaked in the wind, the sound pealing like a faulty chime. Abe grasped at her waist. She resisted, turning away from him. They had no money. What would they do now? She had no idea and she waited to hear his solution. 'Ach,' he said finally, rubbing at his eyes with the balls of his hands. 'We need to find some of our own people, until we can get help from America or Rietavas.' Shameless enough to ask for more help from his stinking liquorice cousins, Sasha thought. He would never be able to stand on his own two feet.

Downstairs they found the landlady unblocking the kitchen sink, a rubber plunger pressed down on the plughole, a rancid food smell brooding in the room. 'There are some Yiddisher kops in this city?' Abe asked the woman, curt in his anxiousness.

'Jewish peoples,' Sasha explained, remembering words from childhood synagogue sermons. Many pious Jews would stop in Rietavas on their way to the site of Rabbi Nachman's grave for Rosh Hashanah. Often the exhortations, even for the children, were delivered in three languages. The landlady frowned at them, expression bordering on fear, the plunger swinging at her knee. Sasha thought of something. She turned the lapel of her blazer back, showing the landlady the gold macramé Star of David sewn there, a secret Bat Mitzvah gift from her mother. In Orthodox Jewish households girls were not expected to celebrate their coming of age in the way that boys were. Sasha had watched four of her older brothers read Torah aloud at shul and accept gifts of books and money, all the while knowing that her own twelfth birthday would come and go unnoticed. She couldn't raise her voice, or even join in singing zemirot. What was a Jewish girl, but a receptacle for reproduction? Then, just as her twelfth birthday was ending, her mother had sneaked into her bedroom. 'You are a woman now, Sasha,' she'd whispered, handing Sasha the star. Sasha struggled to see what it was, under the weak light from the window. 'You are capable of meaningful and powerful things, like Esther, the Queen.' The exchange so hushed and hurried, as if it hadn't happened at all.

'The packmen up in the valleys?' the landlady said.

It seemed the three of them had reached some kind of understanding. Abe nodded zealously. 'There are a few of them up there,' the woman continued, 'in the mountains fifteen miles north, tailors and the like. You take the Taff Vale Railway, around the corner from here; I'll walk you.' The woman took an overcoat from the stand in the hall, slipping into it as she opened the front door, inviting the couple to follow her out into the street. Abe took the trunk from the foot of the stairs, dragging it over the threshold, glad to be making some kind of progress.

A northern-bound passenger train was chugging toward the platform as they reached the station entrance. 'Go, go, go,' the landlady yelled at them, panicked. There were only two trains going that way every day and she didn't want to be lumbered with them and their domestics a second night. American money would keep until she could exchange it at the international bank on Friday. British coins she could use that afternoon. Sasha helped Abe mount the trunk into the carriage since it took the two of them to lift it off the ground. She stared out at the terracotta building as the train began to move, the guard blowing his whistle. 'Not Ellis Island after all,' she sniped. It was cruel but she couldn't resist. She should have been in Rietavas, resting, not scared to death in a foreign country she'd never planned on visiting. They waved at the landlady then found a seat and settled down; a heavy-lidded, hollow-cheeked man on the opposite seat watching them furtively. 'Up to the valleys to make your fortune, is it?' he asked. Neither Abe nor Sasha understood the question. They smiled back at him blankly; hands clasped in their laps. It was forty minutes later that the landscape began to alter, the rounded green hills turning to steep black pyramids jutting at wild, unfathomable angles. Below them were the outskirts of a township, row houses snaking up and down, back and forth, a chapel, an ironmonger, above them a few skinny trees that seemed to teeter backward, ashamed of the view. Abe pointed out a cockle-seller, and then a second man pushing a bicycle, its handlebars draped with long strings of onions.

'Fares please, sir. Fares?' A man in uniform stood in the aisle, waiting for Abe's payment. Abe, guessing what the man was after, reached into his shirt pocket for the American money, offering him the last two notes. The man in uniform frowned into Abe's hand. 'You don't have any English money? Six shillings?' Abe offered the dollars a second time, unable to understand why the landlady had accepted his money but this stupid putz would not. 'Bloody vagrants,' the hollow-cheeked man said to the guard, eyeing Abe and Sasha sideways. 'Bloody nuisances they are, you can't breathe here for gypsies these days. Throw them off I would.' He shrugged once then turned away, fiddling with the buttons on his coat. The guard spoke to Abe a third time. 'If you don't have the legal tender, I have a duty to put you off.' The train was slowing into a station and he squinted out of the window before taking one last look at Abe's vacant face. 'Right you are,' he said, lugging the couple's trunk from underneath their seat. He cast it out onto the platform, ordering Abe and Sasha out after it, the heavy-lidded man not looking up from his lap.

Sasha noticed the damp sulphurous smell of the place before she'd stepped onto the platform. It was noisier here than in the city; with a thundering mechanical drone of tram cars and winding mechanisms. Just when she thought it couldn't get any louder an invasive trumpet-like alarm rang through the town, giving her a twinge in her belly. Her waters broke, a dark pool of liquid spilling into the gaps between the dogtooth tiles. Abe noticed before she did. 'Oy,' he yelled running to the station entrance, gesticulating madly at passers-by. Sasha slumped to the ground, fear paralysing her legs, the view of her husband obscured by diesel smoke. A coal train was darting along the opposite track, containers heaped with small mountains of the shiny black substance. The fast clackety-clack rhythm of it was immense, the containers never-ending. It seemed to hypnotise her, her vision blurring. Quickly she lost consciousness.

When she woke up she was on a stretcher, Abe and two strange, quarrelling women carrying her through the high street. The first woman was a big lady in a velveteen dress, a nursing cap on her head, the second younger and undernourished, wearing stockings and winkle-pickers. 'Just who do you think you are?' the first one bellowed over Sasha's supine body. 'Walking these streets in your whore's get-up? Time and again I tell you

Rosie Griffiths, this is not that kind of town. You want to play your two-bit floozy games, you go to the docks. Next time I catch you at it I'll bring the police to you, I swear it.'

'And who made you the authority, Lilly Pugh?' the second woman yelled back. 'Village midwife is all that you are and rumour has it you failed your midwifery test anyway. I've got a cousin near the examination centre in Somerset. Bet you didn't know that, did you?' She let go of the stretcher to adjust one of her curls, pinning it securely to her head. Abe took the extra weight. 'It's women like you that drive their husbands into my arms, stiff and cold as fish.'

Sasha must have drifted off a second time. The next thing she knew she was on a bed in a tiny, bare room, the woman with the nursing cap sat in the corner watching her, Abe nowhere to be seen. 'There you are,' the woman said. She stood up, working her way along a narrow fissure towards Sasha. She reached to touch the girl's forehead but Sasha recoiled, glimpsing the gold crucifix hanging from the woman's fatty neck.

'What?' the woman asked, offended. She held the crucifix in thumb and forefinger. 'Not a vampire are you, my lovely girl?'

Sasha looked around for the blazer and the macramé Star of David in order to explain herself. It wasn't holy to pray in the presence of a crucifix and she felt that right now, she needed to pray. The blazer was gone. She was wearing somebody else's white nightdress.

'Helping you out I am, gul,' the woman said. 'Didn't have to, neither. You'll be in a better mood when I get back, or I'll put you where I found you, back out on the street.' The woman left the room, adjusting her nursing cap as she went. It was only then that Sasha seemed to notice the pain; an agony washing through and over her like a pulse, a punctual spasm that lifted her a few inches off the bed. She writhed and whimpered, her forehead prickled with a malarial sweat. It was impossible to measure time. She didn't know how many minutes had passed when Abe appeared, the white strings of his prayer shawl tangled, coat and yarmulke rain-dappled. 'Where have you been?'

'Walking the streets like a waif because that damn nurse won't let me in here,' he told her. 'I've been looking for work.' He'd been drinking schnapps again Sasha reckoned, dark half-circles under his eyes. 'You found some?' she asked him, suspicion plain in her voice. 'No,' he said. 'How could I? The Jews here peddle wares. I have no money for materials, no outlay. Oh vez mear. So close to an easy life at the Milstein Kosher Liquorice Company.'

'Now is not the time for self-pity, Abe,' Sasha jeered at him. 'I am in real pain.'

'You think I don't know it? The whole village can hear your shrieking, louder than the tram cars. The beauty of a woman is in her silence, bubbeleh.'

'I am in labour you dumb idiot.' Sasha kneed him in the small of his back. Abe dropped his head into his hands, suddenly miserable. 'You are right, Sasha,' he said, his voice a drunken bawl. 'I am an idiot, nothing but a useless idiot. I bring my family to a foreign country where I cannot provide for them. I am weaker than a housecat. All I ever wanted was to be a successful man, a vendor at the Milstein Kosher Liquorice Co.'

'Out.' The midwife was standing in the doorway, a bowl of borscht in her hands, steam curling from it. 'Out!' she shouted at Abe, threatening to tip the hot soup into his lap. 'I will not have you in here, upsetting my patient. Get out of here.' Abe frowned incredulously at the woman. He was the father of the baby and still she spoke to him like this? She put the bowl down on the bedside table. 'Good Welsh cawl,' she said to Sasha. 'Build you up nice and strong.'

'Do not eat it!' Abe warned his wife. 'It's not kosher. It's forbidden.'

Sasha shrugged. She was hungry. What other option was there?

'Get out!' The woman turned, slapping Abe across the back of his head, pushing his yarmulke to a slant. She frogmarched him to the door, slamming it in his face. 'Men!' she said to Sasha. 'Worse than kids.' Sasha understood what the midwife was saying. The Yiddish for children was kinder. She smiled anew at the lady, ready to comply, but the lady didn't notice. She only scrambled under the blanket, swiftly inspecting Sasha's most private parts. 'Still a few hours left, gul,' she said, coming up. 'Rest for a while. I'll come back at sundown.'

At the Pugh house at the northern edge of the Welsh mining village, Lilly set the kitchen table, ladling the remainder of her beef cawl into three shallow bowls. Her husband and adolescent son were arriving back after their shift at the Lewis Merthyr Colliery, hobnail boots stamping on the linoleum. 'Come here and eat first,' she shouted to them. Usually she'd have them bathe in the parlour before she'd look their way. She hated to see them so filthy: squalid moleskin trousers making a mess of the dining chairs, their skin black with coal dust, only their eyes and lips left untainted, as if they'd somehow been turned inside out. 'I've had fun and games today,' she said as the men congregated at the table, sitting down either side of her. 'That tramp Rosie Griffiths knocking here telling me there's a greener woman delivering on the station. There bloody was as well. I've got her in the Golden Key boarding house. I have to go back at eight. How was your day, you two?'

'Bad one,' her son said. He grabbed a slice of the white bread, folding it in half, stamping his fingerprints on the coarse dough. 'Hell of a lot of muck,' he said biting down on it. 'You have many Jews down there?' Lilly asked her husband, her voice turned sugar-coated. Ivor Pugh slurped at his soup. 'A few on the coke ovens,' he shrugged. Then, realising what she was really asking he said, 'A few more over the other valley. Send them that way.' He was forever begging the foreman for work for his wife's new arrivals. He'd been warned about it twice already. There were more foreigners than there were jobs. 'But straight off the boat. Hardly a word of English between them,' Lilly exaggerated. 'They're scared, love. Poor bloke's running about the streets like a blue-arsed fly. Take him with you in the morning. See if he can't do a few days.'

'Lilly!' Ivor stared through the window at the tip, the endless honey-combing from the pit-work going on beneath them. He wanted to be up on the tump with the other men, taking some fresh air. 'It's the only way I'll get paid,' Lilly said. There was that, Ivor supposed. And the foreman was his brother. How could he say no? 'My old kit's still in the cwtch,' their son said. He'd changed positions a few days earlier, moving from the coke ovens to the mineshaft. 'So there we are then,' said Lilly, as if it was that easy.

At the boarding house the baby was half-out, its head and left fist, like a human jack-in-the-box, dangling between Sasha's splayed legs, an unhealthy forget-me-not blue. Sasha was despondent, refusing to strain, her eyes fixed stubborn on a dint in the top of the wall. Abe paced the landing. 'Get me a tin bath,' Lilly said, surveying the scene as she arrived. 'Lukewarm, not too hot.' Still wearing her raincoat she crawled up onto the bed, rolling Sasha onto her side. She squatted on the girl's hip, pushing her weight onto the baby. She massaged the pelvis with bent knuckles. 'Ach,' Sasha blurted, shocked by the midwife's tactics. There was a sudden movement in her womb.

'Got her,' the midwife said. She moved down the bed, catching the baby with a bloody slap. Abe spied through skinny fingers from the doorway. 'It's a girl,' the midwife announced before the baby started up wailing. 'The bath?' she asked Abe. But Abe was dumbstruck, holding onto the doorframe, bilious and inept. 'Well, bloody hell,' Lilly said. 'I'll get it myself.' She propped the baby on Sasha's chest, blood saturating the girl's nightdress. 'Up early for you in the morning, mind,' she said, prodding at Abe's chest as she headed out of the room.

She pointed at the clock on the wall. 'Starting work at the colliery you are.'

At 5.15 a.m. the next morning, Abe was half-awake, had been the same way all night, the baby's crying relentless. 'Trust God to give me a daughter,' a thought half-formed in his bleary head. She'd stopped now he noticed. He turned cautiously to examine his wife and new child; Sasha asleep, sitting up, the baby dozing in her lap. He heard the echo of footsteps in the street below and a knock on the front door. He froze to listen, rapt. The footsteps came into the house and up the stairs. He sidled out of the bed, going to the landing in his underwear, his legs tired, footsteps shaky. A broad, moon-faced man was leaning patiently against the banister, a pair of boots pegged in his hands. Abe noticed the scars on his red cheeks, blue threads, like smudged ink. He dropped the boots to the floor, the thud reverberating along the skirting board. 'Put them on,' he said.

Abe did what he thought he was being told to do. He dressed and followed the man down the stairs, perplexed, yet glad to be leaving the bedroom and its awful smell of blood, like copper and iron filings. Abe was getting a feel for strangers these days. He could tell their intentions by the way their eyes landed on his face. Some people would look only at his aquiline nose, refusing to meet his gaze, like the conman back in Klaipéda, the crew on the ship. Others, like the drunkard who'd insisted on buying him brandy at the tavern yesterday, locked pupil on pupil, trying to penetrate the language barrier by going straight for the soul. He wouldn't be duped again.

Outside the stars glistened in a clear sky, frost gleaming on the far off fields he and Sasha had seen from the train. He could hear water burbling but the morning was too murky to let him see the river or brook that produced it. The boots pinched like teeth but Abe followed the man obediently along the street. They came upon a narrow lane leading to a railway siding, getting closer to the winding gear wheel that dominated the village. The man turned to him, nodding decidedly. 'Here we go,' he seemed to be saying, and Abe braced himself for whatever was going to be his fate. He recognised the profiles of other men working diligently in the distance, shovelling slag into a tramcar. And then, rising out of the ground mist on the mountain behind them, a larger group of men stood in a sombre, haphazard semicircle, white ribbons hanging at their thighs resembling the strings of his own prayer shawl. He thought he heard the faint rumble of Hebrew blowing off the hill, scattering in the air above him like sparks from a Catherine Wheel. He stopped to count the men: ten. 'A minyan?' he asked a-gasp.

The moon-faced man nodded casually. It was something he'd seen before.

'Yids?' Abe asked. 'Of Europe? Europe Yids?'

'Poland,' the man said.

'Baruch Hashem!' said Abe, his voice swell with gratification. A minyan. A miracle. 'Mazel Tov. Mazel Tov.'

By May Abe and Sasha and the new baby Yocheved had moved into living quarters above the drapery on the eastern fringe of the village. Sasha helped with the repairs using a lockstitch machine left by the previous occupant, an old lady who'd been sent to a mental institution. Abe was working in the coke ovens with the Poles. The terrible hooter blast that had sent Sasha into premature labour was now a source of comfort, notifying her of the end of her husband's shift. He could not sneak off to the tavern without her knowing about it. 'You know why the Welshmen are so short?' he'd say when he arrived home, his Tommy-box tucked under his arm. 'Squatting down in the dark all day, it stunts their growth. Still,' he'd rub his hands together as he sat down to eat his matzo balls, 'won't be long until we've saved enough for our passage.' He'd written to Levi begging for his position to be left open until he could travel to New York. 'I'll be a vendor for the profitable Milstein Kosher Liquorice Company yet!'

On the morning of the second Pesach Sasha was winding the baby when through the window she saw a telegram boy entering into the shop below. He came up the stairs to the flat asking for a signature for the cable. It was addressed to Abe, from America, the ornate Milstein Kosher Liquorice Company insignia printed in the top right corner. She steamed open its seal on the hot breath of the kettle. 'Dear Sir,' it said, 'we do regret to inform you that-' Sasha guessed the next part, but read it anyway; 'the famous Milstein Kosher Liquorice Company has become the subject of a voluntary liquidation requested by Mr L. and Mr I. Milstein of Cherry Street, the Tenement District. Please address all future correspondence to the Division of Corporations at the Department of State, New York.'

'The Milstein Kosher Liquorice Co.,' Sasha sighed sadly. She was on the cusp of scrunching the telegram into a ball, when instead she decided to leave it on the table for her husband to see. When Abe got home and sat down, he gave the letter a cursory glance. 'You see?' Sasha said. 'You see how well your booze-fuelled cousins are doing?' Abe shrugged his shoulders defensively. He stabbed a dumpling with the prongs of his fork. 'Doesn't matter,' he said resigning himself too easily to the news. 'I'm starting my own company with the Yids from the coke ovens anyway.'

'Oh yes?' Sasha asked sarcastically.

'Yes,' he said. 'We're going to be pack traders. We're going to put our money into a syndicate and buy our stock from the city. We'll sell it door to door. That's the way. That's the thing. That's what all the Yids are doing.'

'The new thing?' Sasha said.

'I'll be a vendor for myself,' he said.

'A vendor for himself,' Sasha said to Yocheved, bouncing her on her hip.

'The Milstein Kosher Vending Co.' said Abe.

Little Loosie Mulrooney

You're sitting idle, waiting, in the booking area of the George Motchan Detention Centre when the guard, Ms. Jones, appears. 'What're you doing here again, Lawrence?' she asks as she rifles through your paper grocery bag, noting your personal possessions down in the record book. Her skin is the darkest shade of black, giving off a shiny blue hue in the milk-white tiled room. You shrug as she pats you down, searching for contraband. You've nothing on you: the cops have already taken the carton of cigs from your backpack. 'You get caught again?' she says.

She knows damn well you got caught again. It's all there in the report on your arrest. 'Yes, I did, Ms. Jones,' you say just to be polite.

'Well, well, well,' she says, her voice high and sing-songy as if she's talking to an animal, or a child. 'Little Loosie Mulrooney; picked up again.' You scratch at the rash on your wrists. It's all over you, like measles. It's been there for four days now, tingling so bad you want to rip your skin off. You're scrawbing like a crack-head, making yourself bleed. 'I need to see a doctor, Ms.,' you say, showing her the scabs on your forearms.

She looks at them as if they're going to jump right off and land on her. 'Damn,' she says, stepping backwards. 'That contagious?'

You shrug your shoulders. You don't know. Truth be told, you're worried about it. That's why you didn't run too fast when you first noticed the plain clothes cop traversing 8th and 35th. You've been acquiring free medical care courtesy of Rikers Island for two years or thereabouts. 'Best we get you over to West Facility to get you checked out,' she says going for the phone. It's quare; the closest thing you have to a Ma here in America is a black penitentiary guard.

The doctor is new, a young Philippine. He inspects your cankers through a magnifying glass. 'Do you play any close contact sports?' he asks. 'Wrestling? Football?' You shake your head. 'Impetigo,' he says commandingly. 'It's a bacterial skin infection, common amongst children and highly contagious. You'll have to stay here in confinement until it's cleared. You'll need a course of antibiotics, a few applications of hydrogen peroxide.'

'Thank you, Jesus,' you think to yourself. You've stayed in the Taylor houses before. The last time you were here a correctional officer gave you a black eye for being Irish and you fear there's a lot worse to come. The doctor goes, leaving you to contemplate the notepad on the desk, the kind that came from a pharmaceutical rep, a picture of a green and yellow capsule printed in the corner. Two nurses arrive now, dressed like beekeepers. They instruct you to strip butt naked and lie down on the hospital bed. They paint your crusty body with a creamy camomile-scented lotion which stings for a second, then melts the furious itching that's been driving you madder than bat shit. 'Thank you, Jesus,' you think to yourself when they deposit you in a 6 x 8ft cell, a clean set of orange coveralls folded on the cot.

You know that drugs are what makes the world go around, that addiction is where the money is. You began to form this opinion back in Limerick City, two summers ago. Sure, you should have listened to the Jesuits at your high school, who told you you could do worse than follow your good Uncle Micheál into the priesthood, or your Da, who fancied you a stone-layer like himself. But your heart wasn't in those things. Your heart was in foostering about. You liked your Playstation. You liked getting stocious in the Wicked Chicken on a Friday night. It was one of those Friday nights that you met O'Sullivan, a runner for the Dundon-McCarthy faction on the Ballinacurra housing estate. He was eighteen, like yourself, but he drove a series 1 coupé to the Hyde Road post office to draw his dole. They offered you a little trafficking job all of your own, which was a glamorous way of describing a pretty ordinary stroll up to the old city, a plastic grocery bag in your hand. You didn't mind at all; that part of Limerick took you by Burger King, where a girl with a tongue piercing called Róisín Aherne worked. You'd a crush on Róisín that turned your bones to strawberry jam and on your way home you'd stop for fries and a drink and you'd tremble like a dead leaf on a deciduous tree when she passed by wiping at the Formica table tops.

A few months after you'd got the job you were at home in O'Curry Street, watching Coronation Street with your Ma, when an Audi with blacked-out windows pulled up outside, sounding its horn. It was a senior member of the Dundon gang, a big feller in a Manchester Utd jersey, your boss in effect, along with a few lads your own age, including O'Sullivan who was wearing a pair of black wraparound shades. They said they were taking you out on your first hit. You noticed the butt of the Glock semi-automatic poking out from under the seat. You'd a terrible feeling about it in the pit of your gut but you went along with it because that was easier, sitting in the back next to O'Sullivan, a stiff, fake smile on your mug. Your Man U feller headed along Dock Road and up onto the Island where the rival Keane-Collopy gang were based. He drove around and around until the light had faded, the sun casting a macabre shadow over the pyramids of rubbish piled up against the medieval walls. 'Who are you looking for?' you asked him, because you were sick of the elephantine silence in the hot, airless car.

'Gobdaw called Marc Kelly,' came the answer. 'Friend of Collopy's. We've orders so.'

The car was crawling past a pub on the edge of the estate when four run-of-the-mill-looking lads came stumbling out of the door, floundering along the curb. ''Tis him! There!' O'Sullivan yelled, pointing at one of them. 'Fecker in blue at the back.' The boy on the other side of you went for the pistol, aiming it out of the window. He fired it four times, each shot pushing poor Kelly further up against the wall, like gusts of some supernatural wind. There was no blood at first. When Kelly slumped to the floor the boy with the gun jumped out of the car, shooting him in the head at close range, the three other fellers running for their lives down the dark alleyway.

'What a craic!' the kid said as he jumped back into the car. The senior man put his foot on the gas and headed for the Broad Street Bridge. You kept looking out of the back window, expecting Kelly to get up, because how could a fit lad like himself be so alive one second, and so dead the next?

The Dundon-McCarthy gang took you to a house party in Ballinacurra to celebrate your initiation. Sure, you didn't feel like celebrating. Your jaw was throbbing from all of the fake smiling, and the vodka and cocaine only seemed to make it feel worse. 'Have another hit,' the lad who shot Kelly said, handing you the straw. 'Hit?' he said, elbowing you jocularly. 'Hit? D'ya get it?' His laugh had no laugh in it, just a wheeze; thiss-thiss-thiss, like the snake from *The Jungle Book*. Suddenly you felt sick but you'd no time to make it to the bathroom. You threw up over your T-shirt, a spurt of clear, acidic liquid. 'I want ta go home now,' you blurted, not thinking too clearly.

'To yer Mammy?' O'Sullivan japed. 'Little Larry wants ta go home to his Ma!' You took offence to him calling you 'little', even though everyone called you 'little' from the time that you were born. You thought that the drugs were making you paranoid. You needed to clear your head. You got up and went to the front door but before you caught hold of the handle there was a paw clamped on your shoulder. You saw the reflection of the Man Utd feller in the patterned glass, his ink-black eyes bulging out of his head. 'Where d'ya think you're off ta, Mulrooney?' he asked you.

'I'm sick and me Ma'll be worrying,' you whimpered, too terrified to think up a lie. Your answer seemed to satiate him. He let go of you, stepping back. 'You won't be an eejit now, will yer?' he said, 'Go flapping your gums where they're not needed.'

You shook your head: a reflex, like your body was on its own auto pilot.

'Ginger Collins was an eejit,' the feller said. 'He told the wrong person the wrong thing. You remember what happened to Ginger Collins, ey?'

Ginger Collins was a twenty-year-old lad the Gardai'd found buried in a shallow grave next to the railway line a month earlier. You'd read about it in the *Limerick Leader*; how he'd probably been made to dig the grave himself. The story had made you shudder but you hadn't dwelled on it too long because you thought Ginger Collins was one of the kingpins in the Dundon-McCarthy faction, and that you were just a kid at the bottom, earning yourself a crust; that although you both worked for the same people, you revolved around different planets. Now, under the harsh red sodium lights of the estate, you weaved through the alleyways towards the city, knowing this was no longer the case.

The next day you woke in a pool of cold sweat, having

made a decision in your sleep. You had to leave Limerick. You rang your Uncle Micheál at his apartment near the St. Catherine of Genoa Church in Brooklyn, New York. You'd always liked your Uncle Micheál because he used to build boats from dismantled orange crates and sail them with you on the muddy bank of the Shannon, behind the Hunt Museum. You told him that the financial situation in Ireland was a heap of shite; that you'd been looking for a job for eighteen months and you hadn't even got an interview at the O'Connell Street branch of Abrakebabra. It was four in the morning in the Big Apple. He was cranky. But he said he thought he could add you as a dependant on his Religious Worker Visa. 'When are you thinking of coming?' he said, his voice raspy with sleep.

'Today,' you'd told him. 'There's a Continental flight leaving Shannon at one. I'll be at Newark three o'clock your time.'

Unlike your forefathers who'd arrived a century earlier, your first view of America was the rain-drenched macadam of a New Jersey airfield. You needed money so you started work in an Irish pub on Times Square. What got you the job was your fresh Munster burr. The tourists who visit Times Square are exceptionally touristy and the Irish pub is the king of Irish pubs: shamrocks painted on every available surface, including the toilet seats. 'We'll ship you down to our sister establishment on the Lower East when you start to lose your accent,' the manager said. The tipping system was confusing. You were supposed to be polite to all customers, at all times, but nobody told you that. Most of them were a pain in the arse, hicks from the southern states wanting Irish coffees made with bourbon and corned beef and cabbage prepared with collard greens. You kept getting the New York sirloin mixed up with the Gaelic steak. Your colleagues seemed to get more breaks than you because they were smokers who sat on the doorstep out front chugging on American Spirits.

One morning on your way to work you stopped at the kiosk next to the 42nd Street subway exit and bought your own packet of smokes. 'Twelve dollar fifty,' the vendor said throwing them into your open hands. A Latina in a jogging suit, stood browsing the magazine rack, sucked on her teeth. 'They're more expensive than unicorn blood these days,' she said. You didn't know: you'd yet to work out the difference between Euros and US Dollars. You went for your first break before the lunchtime rush started, leaning on the wall of the pub because the cigarette made you dizzy. In the seven minutes it took you to draw it down to the cork, eight people had asked you if you had a spare one that they could take. At the end of the day your pack was empty but you'd only smoked four of them yourself.

At the newspaper kiosk the following day, you bought a second packet of cigarettes. 'Twelve dollar fifty,' the vendor said throwing them down. The guy in the line behind you, a hippy with long, grey fly-away hair said, 'Jeez, Louise, you know smokes are only five dollars a pack in my home state of Virginia?' Every fecker in America seemed obsessed with the price of tobacco. 'How's that?' you asked the man, just to be polite. 'State tax, I guess,' he said. 'Everything's more expensive up here.'

You peeled the cellophane off the packet, smoking the first ciggy on your rushed walk up West 40th, determined to accomplish a habit that'd get you out of the kitchen at regular intervals. 'Hey?' you heard a girl's voice trailing you past the deli's and office buildings. 'Hey handsome, you have a cigarette you could loan me?'

You gritted your teeth as you turned to acknowledge her, an involuntary smile seizing your entire face as you realised she was a juicy; something of the Róisín Aherne in her hazel-coloured eyes. 'I can sell you one,' you told her.

'Sure,' she said riffling in her purse for a banknote while you stared at her mouth, hoping for the glint of a tongue piercing. 'Gimme two loosies for a dollar.' As she turned on her heel you got a whiff of her perfume: a sweet, crisp, cut-grass smell. Somehow it took you straight home, to Limerick in the nineties. It was violent, even then. 'Stab City'. You had to avoid the rugby fellers who liked a jar or seven, and a scrap if their side came off the worse. You'd hear the Kevin Barry ditty sung in the old men's pubs, the collection tins rattling. But the gangs and the drugs – that hadn't started yet. After the school bus dropped you on O'Connell Street you'd go with the O'Doherty lad from Mungret Court, collecting felled apples at the edge of Jackman Park. You'd throw them at the wild ponies on the wasteland behind Colbert Avenue. The old Spratt & Son's paper shop would sell you a single Benson & Hedges for forty old Irish pence. O'Doherty was mad for the fags. His older brother smoked like a Turk and he thought his older brother was the mutt's nuts. You weren't having it: your grandda had his leg off because he'd chain-smoked at the peat-packing factory and your Da said cigarettes were the devil's favourite best friend.

Over the following six weeks you pulled your weight at the Irish pub. You didn't even go out for any cigarettes. You learned the difference between a New York Sirloin and a Gaelic steak. It was only a pot of peppercorn sauce with a dash of Jameson's splashed over the top. To difficult customers demanding food that wasn't listed on the menu, you said, 'No problem at all, sir. No trouble at all.' Your fake smile became imprinted on your face. You suffered a permanent toothache and even the fellers thought that you were trying to pick them up. 'Shrimp instead of clams? No bother at all, sir. The chef'll be happy to accommodate yer.'

Eventually you'd saved enough of your wages to take a train to Virginia. There you found your way to a wholesale tobacco store on the outskirts of Richmond city. The proprietor was an old man who sat at the counter wearing a Coonskin cap, a shotgun propped between his knees, the wall behind him cluttered with photographs of the various tobacco farms situated nearby. You asked him what his best-selling brand of tobacco was. Without missing a beat he pointed at his own pack of smokes, left open on the counter: a menthol cigarette in a tasteful petrol-blue packet. 'Newports,' he said. 'Newports. Even the negroes smoke the menthols.' You bought three cartons of Newports, carrying them to the Amtrak Station in a backpack on your shoulder.

Back in New York you stood on a corner in the middle of Broadway, smoking one ciggy after another, hoping someone would approach you, asking for one. You'd been there for an hour and a half when it started to drizzle, the rain splatters tapping on your forehead getting bigger by the minute. You'd smoked five cigarettes. You were light-headed, sick with the stink of it. In fact you were about to call it a day when a forty-year-old feller in a business suit came out of a Dean & DeLuca, heading straight for you. 'You ain't got one to spare?' he asked you as he fidgeted nervously with his earlobe, his demeanour that of an important person in a rush.

'Seventy-five cents,' you told him. 'Or two for a dollar.' As you spoke a bolt of panic released itself deep in your bowels. You expected him to attack you, mug you, laugh at you, arrest you. 'Sure,' he said thrusting his hand into his trouser pocket, coins jingling. He took two cigarettes and a match before charging down 40th without looking back. Business was slow to begin but by the end of the week you'd gone through your first carton. You'd made a fifty-dollar profit.

Early on Monday morning the following week, you were standing in the spot you'd picked out for yourself on the middle of Broadway when a girl appeared out of the traffic, yelling at you. 'Hey Loosie man,' she said, flushed from running. It was your Róisín Aherne doppelgänger, the dollar bill ready in her hand. 'Thank you, Jesus,' you thought to yourself as your heart leapt into the dish of your mouth. You held onto the newspaper dispenser for balance. 'You're too pretty to smoke,' you told her, your voice reedy with nerves as you handed the ciggies over. 'You'll wreck your lovely skin, so.'

'Oh, I don't smoke,' she said. She pointed one of the cigarettes at you, twirling it in a circular motion, writing an invisible O in the air between you. 'You know what this is? A magic wand, for conjuring cabs.' She jabbed at the ether once with the cigarette. 'You should be charging the earth for these things.' A strange giggling sound came charging from the depths of your voice box, lasting longer than necessary and embarrassing you no end. You struck a match, offering her a light. 'Besides,' she said, her head inclined to take it. 'I'm giving up soon. Why'd you think I'm buying loosies from you, not whole packs from the kiosk?' She blew smoke in your face and you successfully stifled an eye-watering cough. 'You can't smoke anywhere these days anyway.' But she was back again the next morning, and the morning after that.

Fifteen months after quitting your job at the Irish bar to hawk cigarettes on the street, you're sitting in front of the judge at the Midtown Community Court, flanked by Ms. Jones, your guard from the detention centre on Riker's. You suck down a gulp of the cool, air-conditioned breeze as the judge deliberates. 'Your punishment,' he says as you stare at the small pink impetigo scar on the web between your thumb and forefinger. He clears his throat, tapping his gavel on the block. 'Your punishment, Mr. Mulrooney, is a week of community service.'

'Please don't make me sweep the cigarette butts again, sir,' you plead with him. The cigarette butts are horrific. The cigarette butts are never-ending. Imagine it! The street is the only place where smoking is legal. There is no such thing as an ashtray in New York. The last time he made you do it you saw cigarette butts in your sleep for months on end.

'Yes, you're sweeping the cigarette butts again, Mulrooney,' he says. He shrugs callously, fingers pressed on that right earlobe of his. 'It's the most lenient form of discipline considering this is your third time with us.' He puts his hand up as if to block a conversation. 'If you complain again I'll send you back to one of the Taylor Houses.' He stands up with a look of fraught longing on his face, that look you've come to know so well, the look that says its owner is in need of a hard-earned cigarette. Without thinking about it you lift your own hand, going for the loosies in your breast pocket and finding it attached to Ms. Jones wrist, bound by the steel handcuff.

'OK, Lawrence,' Ms. Jones says, misreading your intentions. 'Don't get bent out of shape. You're free to go.' She presses the key into its niche. 'Hang on just one second. Patience is a virtue, you know?'

Holiday of a Lifetime

The blackberries are fresh and bittersweet; releasing a sharp kick when I force and burst them against the back of my teeth. Auntie Lynette is back from the market in Narberth; she's left a punnet for my mother on the worktop. 'You want to wash that muck off your face, gul,' she says watching me slyly as I pick at them. 'You've got more eyeliner on than that bloody Winehouse piece.' I look up from my phone, glaring at the clear plastic patch stuck on her fat, mottled shoulder. I decide to leave her comment go. She's trying to give up smoking; she's in a bad mood.

There's a gush of water as my mother fills the kettle. 'Doctor Gwilym says her body just gave up,' she says, talking now about Auntie Marilyn, who was my real auntie. Lynette is only a neighbour. She lives next door, but she may as well live in our house the way she walks in without knocking, banging on about what I am and am not old enough to do. 'Perhaps she died of a broken heart,' my mother continues, flicking the kettle's switch. 'No apparent reason; it just stopped beating.'

'Have you ever heard such claptrap?' says Lynette; so cynical.

I'm flipping back and forth between recent text messages from Osian and Rhodri, wondering which one of them I should take to the funeral. My mother's said I can take a friend for company, but only one. She's a stingy cow and she reckons the buffet isn't big enough for eleven of us. Osian is my first choice, obviously; dark and lanky. I've just had my braces off and I want to kiss him first. I lick at the enamel of my newly freed teeth, imagining it, envisioning him playing his bass guitar at the school concert, the insides of his forearms milk-white and marbled with raised blue veins, his dog tags glinting beneath his shirt collar. But I know in my gut that I should pick Rhodri; ginger and thickset, polite and well behaved.

'It'll be that inbred with his black magic,' Lynette says. 'You know what they're like.' It takes me a few seconds to work out who she's talking about. Marilyn had made friends with one of the gypsy men from the Westover site a few years back. Lynette was adamant they'd been sleeping together, that the gypsy'd been after Marilyn's money. The council has evicted most of them this summer. There are only six caravans left.

'Well, the coroner says there's no explanation,' my mother says. 'They've recorded the death as exhaustion.' Lynette pulls her tobacco inhaler from her handbag and sucks on it. 'Nothing but a bunch of thieves,' she says. 'I'll bet my life it was one of them who got hold of my lighter all those years ago, filched it from The Fishers Arms beer garden. They thought it was worth something, I'll bet.'

The memory comes flooding back like molten lava, my heartbeat a bass drum. I shuffle off the top of the washing machine, the blackberry juice dripping down the insides of my fingers, wine red, like menstrual blood. I sit on the settee in the living room, out of sight. Back then Lynette smoked real cigarettes. She'd clog the kitchen up with her yellowy grey fumes. Sometimes it got so thick I couldn't see my way to the fridge. My mother'd go around with a can of air freshener before my father got back from The Fishers, because he didn't like Lynette coming around, putting ideas about new handbags and shoes into my mother's head. This one time, three years ago, I was sat in exactly the same place, eleven years old, listening to them gossiping. Lynette had started a new ciggy, a hiss of gas from her lighter. I loved Lynette's lighter because it was a pistol, an imitation pistol, with a shiny silver barrel and muzzle, and a pretty mother of pearl handle. She'd bought it from a stall in Blackpool and I wanted to borrow it, to take it to school. But Lynette loved her lighter too; because she was a chain smoker it was never out of her sight. I was pressing my head against the radiator. Sometimes I could trick my mother into thinking I was poorly by doing that. I'd keep it there until the heat was too much to stand, my brain warm and pulpy as if it was about to melt and drip from my ear canals like candle wax. 'Ah, Mammy's little princess,' she'd say, baby-talking, brushing the back of her hand against my forehead.

I heard Lynette going for the ashtray on the windowsill, an oyster shell I'd found on Rhossili Beach. 'I saw her,' she said, talking about my Auntie Marilyn, 'in the Ivy House tea room.'

'Oh yes,' my mother said. 'She likes to take her afternoon tea and scone. She thinks she's the bitch's tits, my big sister.' She said 'bitch's tits' in English, her mouth full of spit, as if swearing in a different language wasn't really swearing at all. I distinctly remember wishing that I had a sister just so that I could call her a bitch.

'But that's not it,' Lynette said. 'She was with someone. A boy is all he was, one of them gypsies from off that Westover site. I hate to tell you, really. It's embarrassing for me.' She loved every syllable in that sentence. Then she lowered her voice and I had to tilt my head towards the doorway to hear her. 'French kissing, tongues and everything. And him unshaven and smelling like the trout he's been stealing out of the Tâf.' She sucked on her ciggy.

'Tongues?' my mother asked.

'Aye, looked like. Cosied up in the snug. Canoodling, like.'

Now another memory washes over me like a wave; the time I got the English words *canoodling* and *canoeing* mixed up. I was on a daytrip to Cenarth with Rhodri and his father when I saw an old feller in a little wooden boat, sailing down the river towards us. 'Look,' I said, pointing. 'There's a man there canoodling.' Rhodri laughed so hard he dropped his ice-cream in his lap, the raspberry sauce and sprinkles of hundreds and thousands sticking to his trousers. Gwynfor tutted. 'Technically,' he said spitting on a hanky he'd whipped from his pocket, 'they're coracling. Those boats are called coracles; traditional Welsh fishing boats.'

After Lynette's French kissing revelation, I had trouble trying to imagine Auntie Marilyn with one of the dirty gypsies from the Westover site. It was like Marilyn was chocolate cake and the gypsy was corned beef gravy. You couldn't put them in the same bowl. Besides, I knew that Marilyn still loved Uncle Elvis. Derek had died two years earlier. We called him Elvis because after a few pints he liked to sing 'Are You Lonesome Tonight?' on the karaoke in The Fishers. He had a white silk jumpsuit and glue-on sideburns. Every year he competed in an Elvis competition down south. They played 'Are You Lonesome Tonight?' at his funeral and Auntie Marilyn collapsed, smashing her knees on a marble gravestone. After that we found out he'd gambled their lifesavings away. My mother told me that he'd donated the money to the bookmakers in Llanelli because he liked watching the racehorses going round and round the track. D'uh. Auntie Marilyn moved into my grandparents' bungalow on the edge of the Cwmllan woods. 'She's only staying there temporary,' my mother said. Because really the bungalow was ours, and my mother's a stingy cow.

She wasn't on good terms with Marilyn because of the way Marilyn had acted after my last Nativity Play in the junior school. My mother was excited because I was playing Mary and on the night my voice was loud and clearer than Angelina Carter's from Meadow Croft. Rhodri was Joseph and Osian the innkeeper. When

Rhodri and I approached the little cardboard prop inn at the edge of the stage, Osian appeared, his arms folded, his face spiteful. He stared at me, then at Rhodri. 'Mary can come in,' he said, 'but Joseph can eff off.' I wasn't worried but in the car on the way home my mother told me not to worry. 'Osian is jealous,' she said, 'because Rhodri got a bigger part.' Suddenly Marilyn cackled, loud and crazy as a shithouse rat, slapping her legs over and over. 'Ten years old and effing and blinding like a good 'un,' she said.

'What's the matter with you?' my mother hissed at her. 'Our Lleucu practiced long and hard for that part. It's not funny. It's a bloody disgrace. That's what comes of divorce, that is. Kids who need their mouths washed out.'

'Oh, you mollycoddle her, gul. There's no harm done.'

'What would you know about it?' my mother spat. 'You never had any kids.' And that was the start of their not talking, which has lasted until now, all because of Osain, wicked, stunning bastard that he is.

On the first day of the summer holidays between junior school and comprehensive, I got up and poured my cereal. I was going in the fridge for the milk when I heard my mother crying in the downstairs bathroom. The door was open; my mother sitting, trousers-up on the toilet, pulling tissue paper from the toilet roll dispenser to wipe at her pink and blotchy face. 'That sister of mine's a liability,' she said, talking to the shaggy blue mat on the floor. 'Merry as the day is long and selfish as a fox.'

'Mam,' I said, to show her that I was there. She looked

at me, but with no recognition in her face. She chose a spot on the wall behind my shoulder and started bawling again. 'To think of her rutting around with a teenager, a gyppo no less, and her poor Derek, still warm.' The toilet paper came to an end, the cardboard carcass spinning. I'll have that later, I thought, to make a toilet roll spaceship. 'She's already had her share,' my mother said. 'She had the car and the savings. Oh, she had to spend it, didn't she? On a luxury cruise of all things. "Holiday of a lifetime", she said. Holiday of a flaming lifetime! Well the house is mine. She'll lose it, I swear. They'll trick her they will. It's easy enough. Where's my holiday of a lifetime? Even Lynette goes to Blackpool once a year.'

She hadn't been on holiday since she'd married my father. She still hasn't. It's all she ever goes on about, that and the handbags and the shoes. But I know she doesn't really want to go on holiday because once when my father suggested she go away with Auntie Lynette she said she'd rather do a shift in the fish shop than go to God-awful Blackpool. 'That's not the kind of holiday I'm talking about, Lionel,' she said, snapping at my father. 'I'm talking about Crete, the Balearics, the Med somewhere, I don't know.'

'I'm hungry, Mam,' I said, bored and going back to my cereal. When I actually got to open the fridge, that's when I saw it from the corner of my eye: a sunray bouncing off the polished cylinder. Auntie Lynette had left her lighter on the windowsill. It was there – big as tomorrow, sat next to the old oyster shell. I got a foothold in the washing machine door and stretched up, reaching for it. It was light, and simultaneously heavy, a jewel in my little hand. I stroked the pearl inset with two fingertips, the feel of it smooth and hard against my skin. My mother was moving around in the bathroom, the tap running. I slipped the pistol into my gingham dress pocket. Three thoughts came to me, very quickly, one after the other. I couldn't take the gun to school because the school was closed. I couldn't take the gun to Osian's house because Osian had gone to his father's place in Trimsaran. It might have been my only chance to borrow the gun, to show it to somebody, so I decided to take it to Marilyn's on the edge of the Cwmllan woods. And maybe, if the gypsy was there, the gun would scare him away.

To get to Llandewi Velfrey I had to go along West Street and past the Westover Caravan Park where the gypsies had set up camp. They'd been there for five months, their rubbish piling up next to the outer wall. I could see a mattress and a heap of black bags long before I got anywhere near. Later we found out it was the Evans family from St. John Street who'd been fly tipping the rubbish, but back then I was scared of the caravan site, mainly because Auntie Lynette kept telling me that if they caught me the gypsies would steal the gold out of my teeth. I could hear the kids screeching in their funny accents; English with a strange twang that sounded like they had a handful of gravel in their gobs. 'Twt lol,' my mother called it: gobbledygook. They were playing; riding a cob horse saddle-less, from one side of the field to the other. I was sad that Osian had gone to Trimsaran, and that we couldn't play cowboys with Lynette's lighter, and that I wasn't allowed to play with him anymore anyway because he was from a broken home, and suddenly I wanted to turn back, but I couldn't, in case Lynette had come around looking for her pistol lighter.

It turned cold when I got off the main road and onto the narrow country lane leading to the house, the tall hedges blocking the sunlight. My shins had turned to gooseflesh and I was thirsty as a goldfish that'd jumped out of its bowl. I remember thinking specifically about a goldfish that'd jumped out of its bowl because the school goldfish had jumped out of its bowl on the last day of term and Rhodri'd had the blame because he was on goldfish duty. I was hoping that Marilyn had Coca-Cola because usually people without kids only had tea or coffee, squash if you were lucky. I got to the stone grit-dispenser and noticed it was shaped like a coffin. It was there so that Marilyn could sprinkle rock salt on the ice in the winter. I knew that, I must have, because I'd been there a few months earlier with my father to deliver the rock salt. But because of what it was shaped like I couldn't help thinking that the gypsy had killed someone and hidden them inside. Osian had been telling me vampire stories. He loved telling me vampire stories. I walked so fast I got a stitch but I didn't stop until I saw the pink shingles of the bungalow through the gaps between the elm trees.

The fishing flies that my grandfather collected had gone from the drainpipe on the veranda where he tacked them, their fuzzy, luminous wings fluttering in the wind, belying the razor-sharp fish hooks hidden inside. A row of drooping sunflowers bordered the house, their leaves twisted and brown. I crept up the steps and onto the veranda, going to the window, my hands shaped into binoculars. The window was smudged with Auntie Marilyn's cat's paw prints. It took a while for my eyes to adjust. Then I saw her, lying on her settee, her long skirt hitched up to her thighs. Her legs were white and lumpy with purple varicose veins. The gypsy was standing up, almost touching the low ceiling, the beginning of a faint black moustache on his upper lip, a waxy fisherman's coat around his shoulders. I must have gasped as he kneeled down adjacent to Marilyn's bare legs. He began to rub something, some ointment into her swollen knees, his hands slow and gentle, Marilyn's eyelids heavy, a half smile on her orange lips.

The floorboards on the other side of the veranda creaked. I stepped back, my guts in my mouth. A gypsy boy was slumped on the step in front of the door, his face partially hidden behind the sunflower leaves. He opened his eyes, surprised, and sat up straight, his dark hair clipped to the skull apart from three knotty rat tails hanging down to his waist, stiffened with grease. His skin was the colour of tea, except for a silver bruise on the inside of his calf, visible through a huge rip in his dirty blue jeans. 'This isn't your house,' I told him, going tentatively for the pistol in my dress pocket.

The gypsy boy smiled at me, dimples in his cheeks like he'd been stabbed with the point of a compass. 'Going to kill me now, are ye?' he said. He talked so quickly it was hard to work out where one word ended and the other began. It was like he was singing a tune; no lyrics, just a tune, his voice undulating. 'There's no gold in my teeth,' I warned him. As I did I noticed the chinks of gold in his calm, brown eyes, like little shards of honeycomb submerged in milk chocolate. He wasn't really a boy; more like sixteen or seventeen years of age, and something about the way he was looking at me made the pistol seem useless. My face was as hot and clammy as if I'd kept it against the radiator for a whole hour. I dropped the lighter into the depths of my pocket. 'What's he doing to my Auntie Marilyn in there?' I asked him.

'Me broddur?' he said. I nodded though I didn't know what he was asking.

'Me broddur's a horse trainer. He's lookin' at err knees. 'Cause 'err knees're gone stiff like an ole Vanner's. He can soothe 'em so, make 'em well again.'

'That's alright then,' I said though I didn't really understand.

'Where're yer friends, now?' he asked me before lifting a plastic bottle of water to his mouth and drinking a lot of it down.

'Haven't got none,' I said. I didn't mean to say it. It jumped out like *canoodling* had with Rhodri and Gwynfor in Cenarth. I toed the scuffed wood of the veranda, conscious of my own bare shins, expecting the question to drift away. But the gypsy was watching me, waiting for an explanation. 'I was Mary,' I said.

The boy nodded. 'You've a triangular face,' he said. 'Leadership qualities. They'll come around alright; the redhead missing yous already.' How did he know that Rhodri was a ginger? 'How do you know he's ginger?' I asked him. He shrugged. He didn't say anything about

Osian. Osian didn't miss me I realised and at that moment I hated Osian as much as I'd hated anything in my short life, my solar plexus throbbing with sheer fury. The gypsy boy looked at me, his demeanour mild and patient, the sun catching a silver ring on his middle finger and illuminating his dirty, knuckly fingers. A new feeling obliterated the hate, replacing it with an urgent supernatural need in some chasm between my legs. My fingers started to tremble. I retreated down the steps but hoped that he'd call me back. For some reason I wanted to touch his hair, to smooth my fingertips along the length of the rough, rope-like tendrils. I jumped the last step, showing off, and my feet stung as they hit the ground.

'You're not staying to see yer Aunt?' he said.

'Nah.' The thought of his lovely eyes on my bare, bandy legs stopped me from going back, from turning even to peer at him one last time. There was no spit in my mouth, my tongue swollen and cracked. I ran to the main road, my legs numb, the soles of my feet burning with each new step. I stopped at the Pen-lan stream and took a gulp of the cold, fishy-tasting water. I hid Lynette's cigarette lighter under a mossy rock. Closer to home I rubbed a few splodges of mud on my legs so that I could tell my mother I'd been playing rounders on the rugby pitch. But by the time I got to the kitchen, and to Lynette lighting a cigarette off the ring of the gas cooker, I was a different person; too old to play rounders. I went straight to the downstairs bathroom to wash the mud off my legs.

*

Rhodri came to the funeral, wearing a sky-blue suit that Gwynfor'd bought him for last year's football gala. It didn't go with his ginger hair and my mother wasn't pleased, I could tell by her soured face. But she pinned the same Calla Lily buttonhole that our family wore to his lapel, thanking him grudgingly for coming. It could have been worse. It could have been Osian with his luscious new eyebrow piercing. At the reception at the clubhouse, a small group of gypsies form Westover turned up in jogging bottoms and trainers, Lynette staring daggers at them as they lurched to an empty table at the back. I yearned to eyeball the boy I'd met on Marilyn's veranda. I wanted to see his tea-coloured skin, his scraggy dreadlocks. I wanted him to see my straight grown-up teeth, my spray-tanned legs; the way my cleavage bunched in a push-up bra. He wasn't there. He must have belonged to one of the families the council had moved on. The gypsies didn't speak to us. We didn't speak to them. They were first in the queue when the buffet was announced, Rhodri and I at the back. 'Thieves,' Lynette said, fizzing with indignation as she crept up behind us. She glowered at them as they loaded their paper plates with cold pizza.

I wanted to disagree with her but she was still fuming about her simulation pearl pistol lighter. It was too soon to admit I'd taken it without her doing her nut. She was in a bad mood and the news might start her smoking again. I turned to study the gypsies, looking for a redeeming feature I could use in my argument. A dark-skinned, snaggle-toothed boy of eight was cramming handfuls of prawn vol-au-vents into the pockets of his frayed tracksuit.

Highway 77

The tungsten lights above the road sign illuminated the distance loud and clear: Sarita thirty miles. It was the last stop on the main north-south highway to snag immigrants. Tyrone wanted a cup of coffee or another Xanax capsule, something to get him through the ordeal. Already he was shaking, dark sweat patches spreading around the pits of his vest. It was nine in the evening but there was an eerie, morning quality to the light, as if day was about to materialise, fully-formed, like a photograph in developing solution. Calm the heck down, he told himself, his teeth gritted. He'd tell the patrol agents he was running empty and if caught, feign surprise. He'd say they sneaked on while he was asleep in a rest area. It could happen. It happened all the time. As he passed the five mile road sign he rapped on the sleeper compartment three times, the code for keep quiet. The lights of the checkpoint showed up the dead

June bugs flecked on the windshield, the parched scrubland at the side of the road. He steered into line and saw the guard approaching through the mirror. He rubbed at his forehead with his palm, his wiry cornrows turned moist. The metal of the door screeched as the guard turned the handle and stepped up onto the fender. Leaning inside he aimed a flashlight around the cab. 'Where you headed?' he said. 'What you hauling?'

Tyrone let go of his breath, his hand smoothing the back of his neck. 'Houston. I'm empty.'

The flashlight landed on the girl's knees. 'Who's she?'

Tyrone struggled to remember her name. He'd met her less than an hour ago, a runner for Abel. He was giving her a ride to a transaction. 'This here is my girlfriend, sir,' Tyrone said. He could feel his bottom lip trembling. The patrol agent stepped down and closed the cab door, slapping it once before moving along. It had taken less than a minute. Tyrone winked at the girl as he manoeuvred out onto the road.

*

'Brandy,' the girl said. 'My name's Brandy.' The radio had tuned itself into the Vanessa Blessings hour on Kiss FM. A caller from Corpus Christi was talking about dyscalculia, some brain disorder his kid was suffering from. Tyrone was listening to it, oblivious to her. She watched him from the corner of her eye, the way the mast lights reflected green on his huge bicep. He was wearing a gold wedding band on a chain around his neck. What did that mean? That he was separated,

143

divorced? 'I like your freightliner,' she said attempting to initiate conversation. Immediately she wondered if freightliner was the right word. Her granddaddy from Hacienda Heights called them trucker-trailers. When she was little they used to sit on the little balcony of his apartment counting the cars on the Pomona Freeway. She counted red. He counted blue. The first to get to ten won the game. Her granddaddy always let her win; no matter how many cars he counted.

'This old thing?' Tyrone said. He smiled sideways at her, his stretched lips exposing a gap between his right incisor and canine. 'Nothing but a big fridge on wheels.' As an afterthought he added, 'the refrigeration unit's switched off right now.' A dull repetitive thumping sound started up in the sleeper compartment behind them, Brandy feeling the vibration of it through the soles of her ugg boots. Tyrone reached for the radio dial, changing the channel. The disco beat of an old Michael Jackson song fabricated a small balloon of confidence in the pit of Brandy's stomach. 'You know I'm getting a little lonely over here,' she said unhooking her seatbelt. She sidled along the seat until she could feel the seam of Tyrone's denim pants against her bare thigh.

A Fruit of the Loom truck in the adjacent lane hooted at them, the driver gesticulating wildly before the vehicle disappeared into the future. 'What's the matter?' she asked, moving away again slightly, worried.

Tyrone kissed his teeth. 'Those goddamn beaners are up to something. They're screwing up my truck. Shit.'

Tat-tat-tat. He knocked on the compartment wall three times.

Inside the trailer José felt the bracket of a taillight, boxy against his palms. He tore at the insulating fabric with his fingernails until he touched naked metal. He stood up, kicking at it. Two men flanked him so that he didn't fall backwards. 'I've got it,' he yelled as he felt the bracket disembark, his foot hitting air, light and free. He stooped on the floor, the liquid in the layers of sopping clothing squelching under his knees. Some of the passengers had worn three or four layers, avoiding the added burden of luggage. Now the heat was baking everybody up like cornbread. They were pulling their shirts over their heads, peeling their pants from their legs. They could all be naked by now. In the flat-out darkness he wouldn't know.

There wasn't much air coming through the hole in the trailer: the truck was headed in the wrong direction. But by pushing his chin against the split he'd made in the fabric José could almost taste the cold wind on the skin of his lips. He was still for a few moments, thinking about his brother Lorenzo, hard at work in the hog-skinning plant in Iowa. He tried to imagine the house he would share with him when he arrived in Sioux City, a squat white clapboard with a rocking chair on the porch, the stars and stripes flapping in the breeze. Lorenzo never talked in his letters about his digs. Still, that was how José saw it: a white clapboard; a white picket fence. He'd wanted to stay home and make a go of the family pineapple farm in Oaxaca, but productivity was low. It had been for a decade. Lorenzo was gone and his father was too sick to work. His mother earned the majority of the family income, selling fruit candy skulls to the tourists. America was her idea. She sat at the dining table in the evening nursing her sugar burns, talking about the new world as if it was heaven itself. Her voice ascended excitedly as she conjured images of grocery stores stocked to the hilt with canned soups and fine wines, beauty parlours where wealthy Gringo women went to get their fingernails coloured cotton-candy pink, restaurants with crisp white tablecloths and dishes warmed in the oven. All of it she picked up on the black-and-white portable TV in the bar where she sometimes worked a shift, along with a kind American tourist she'd met once when she was a fourteen-year-old girl. She talked until her words ached and winced and José couldn't bear to hear them anymore and he gave in, just like Lorenzo did. Lorenzo had left two years ago on a legitimate tourist visa that he'd never managed to renew. 'You see what a great time he's having?' their mother would say. 'He will never come back! He will never come back and how can I blame him?' She tried to make it sound as if she was disappointed by his absence, but inside she was combusting with pride; everybody knew it.

'Come on boy,' said one of the men standing close to him, voice sharp and eager. 'There are other people here! Other people waiting for air!' Something hit José against the base of his spine. It felt like a hollow tube of metal pipe. He had only boarded the freightliner an hour ago, in a field in the Rio Grande valley. He'd met the other passengers there, hiding under scrub trees, waiting for the truck to arrive. Some he'd met earlier, crossing the river on inner tubes. Already it had come to this: fighting over a worthless breath of fresh air.

*

The air conditioning in the cab up front was broken. Tyrone kept meaning to get it fixed. Summer was coming and the nights held the heat of the day. 'Hot ain't it?' he said. Brandy nodded, taking his question as a cue to remove her ugg boots. She threw them aside and hooked her bare feet on the dash, curling and wiggling her toes, neat squares of purple nail varnish against plump nut brown skin. Brandy's feet were her best feature. A director from Porno Valley had told her so a couple of months back. He was going to use her for the foot fetish market. But she wasn't eighteen yet and the authorities were clamping down on companies using underage actresses. She'd had to borrow money from her granddaddy to come looking for her mom in San Antonio. The last thing she'd heard from her mom was a postcard with the Lone Star Flag, the legend 'Deep in the Heart of Texas' scrawled underneath it. The note said she was working at a beauty salon called Shear Magic on the outskirts of the city. But that was twelve years ago, right after the divorce. It was when Brandy was walking the streets, looking for the salon, that she'd met Abel and he'd given her a gig running dope. The pay was good. After rent there were a few dollars left for new things; a pair of sneakers, a bracelet, and if she was good at it there'd be more work, more things. She could get a car and go back and repay her granddaddy, make it up with her Aunt Maria; make her understand that she hadn't been lying about what Uncle Jim had done. She'd take her Aunt Maria back to the Puente Hills Mall to buy the cute polka dot beach towel that had started the whole quarrel off in the first place.

'Shish.' Tyrone reached up, wiping sweat from his temple with the back of his hand. Brandy stared slyly at the panels of muscle in his upper arms. If she could get a boyfriend to take back to Hacienda Heights with her, someone meaty, and black, like Tyrone, that'd scare the shit out of Uncle Jim. She smoothed her big toe along the edge of the plastic console, moving it in and out of his eye line. He'd begun to watch it furtively when his cell phone started to beep. 'Hey,' he said taking the call.

*

'You have to take them all the way to Houston,' Abel said, a hacking cough bubbling in his throat, releasing itself gradually with the first syllable of every word. He stopped speaking to retch once, and then, 'Otherwise it ain't gonna work out. Extra two thousand bucks in it, man. Cash in hand soon as you hit H-Town.' Tyrone had met Abel at a truck stop two weeks earlier, waiting in line at the register to pay for his steak and cream gravy. 'You headed south?' Abel asked him. He looked like the devil, a red shelf of a forehead, tiny oyster-coloured eyes peering out from underneath. He knew something about him wasn't right. You met all kinds of characters at the truck stops; traffickers, runaway kids, a hunger in their soul that turned their pupils to pinheads. Tyrone avoided them. He was trying to avoid speaking to Abel but the cashier was held up changing the paper roll for the receipts. Besides, Abel was an old man, sixty or thereabout, too old to be any real hassle. He said he had a beaner family with a wrecked-up car needing a ride, that he was buying the car and that he'd give Tyrone a little bit to get the family off the roadside. 'Sure,' Tyrone said. He used this route twice a week, hauling milk from upstate New York to Texas, returning two days later with watermelons. Lately the milk was going west: he was empty. It was only when Tyrone was pulling onto the Highway with the Mexicans in the trailer that Abel threw the wad of cash through the cab window. It was more than Tyrone was expecting. 'Too much,' he said, pulling the handbrake. He searched on the floor for the money to throw it back.

'Take it,' Abel said over his shoulder. He was already headed back to the parking lot. 'They're illegals man. You know that, right? Take the money.'

This time it was eight thousand dollars for driving fifteen of them forty-five miles up the highway. Tyrone needn't go a mile off his usual route. The money was reserved for school fees for his kid up in Philly. Cassie never quit complaining about the inferior standards at his local elementary; she wanted Benji enrolled at the Ad Prima Charter School with its tennis court and debating team and God knows what else. She said he was at risk of repeating his father's mistakes if he didn't get the right education. Tyrone had done a year at the Mira Loma detention centre when he was fifteen for mugging some dumb tourist who'd found his way down to the Watts

Towers, a camera on a strap around his neck. The job had been his initiation into the Crips and the detention centre is where he got his addiction to bench pressing. You had to be fit to survive a week in that place. But that was a different life ago. Cassie had only found out about it when their divorce counsellor let slip a telling comment about the faded eight ball tattoo on Tyrone's shin. She'd thought it was kid stuff until then, some kind of blood-brother thing, and really it was. She never seemed too concerned about Benji's education before that meeting and now her demands were getting more and more absurd: two hundred bucks for a school bag, seven hundred bucks for some rare breed of pet chinchilla. Like Tyrone didn't know it was going towards her collagen jabs and hair extensions. Anyway, where the heck was Benji going to get into gang trouble in goddamned leafy West Oak Lane? That eight grand was going to keep his ex-wife from cutting his balls off every other weekend.

He hadn't seen the immigrants board because Abel said it was best if the passengers never got a look at the driver, in case something went wrong on the road. They were making a hell of a racket and the code wasn't keeping them quiet any more. It sounded like there were way more than fifteen of them back there. He could hear a baby crying, he was sure. Nobody said anything about babies. 'OK, OK,' he said dropping the call.

'Problems?' the girl asked.

'Hmm,' said Tyrone trying to emanate annoyance rather than fear. 'First he asks me to take them to Corpus Christi. Now he wants me to take them all the way to

Houston. That's like six hours or something. Shit.' He pulled into a service station in a ghost town called Refugio and bought three bottles of water. It had to be getting hot in that trailer by now. He walked to the rear end of his vehicle to inspect the damage. They'd kicked the left taillight out. It was hanging from its lonely cable, the hole revealing a cream chunk of foamy insulation material. He forced the first bottle of water through the gap and stood a while, listening. It was quiet as death. He guessed they were sleeping but when he shoved the second bottle through somebody pulled at it.

'How many of you are there?' Tyrone asked.

Hands started clapping on the sides of the trailer, tentative at first and then frenzied, the liner shaking. 'El Niño,' somebody yelled, thrusting their fingers through the cavity. 'El Niño.' Tyrone pushed the third bottle through the hole and went back to the cab. Brandy was leant over the dash, picking at her toenails. He took the Hershey's chocolate bar he'd bought out of his pants pocket, handing it to her. As she took it the whites of her eyes seemed to flicker a few times; a fluorescent light coming on. 'Hey, you know Spanish?' Tyrone asked her. 'What the hell does El Niño mean?' She thought about it as he restarted the engine, the chocolate bar gripped in curled fingers. 'The weather,' she said. 'Or California. I ain't sure. Something about the weather in California?'

*

José bucked and tripped, landing on his knees as the trailer jerked and shuddered. 'The baby!' they were

151

shouting. 'The baby, the baby, the baby!' Others were pounding on the sides of the trailer with shoes and fists; whatever they could get their hands on. As the vehicle started moving again a crowd formed at the tear in the insulation. They were squeezing wet clothing out into the night, hoping to attract attention. José clung to the corrugated floor. A metre away from him the mother and sick baby were wailing miserably, the sound of it unearthly, like something from the ocean. 'Don't cry,' the mother was saying between sobs. 'Don't cry, baby.' The smell was like vomit, a bitter mixture of honey and jalapeño. José's pants were clinging to his legs, heavy with perspiration. He brought the tail of his shirt to his mouth, sucking on the warm, wet, salt-drenched cotton.

'Rock the trailer over,' someone yelled and people began to run at both sides of the liner, their movements cancelling each another out, the trailer swaying fleetingly. There were many other people sitting cross-legged on the floor, like José, nervous, confused.

'Listen,' came a female voice from near the back doors, confident and astute. 'My name is Faviola González-Buendia. I come from Honduras. I am eighteen years old.' José imagined the face of a Spanish movie actress he'd seen on the cover of one of his mother's magazines, sultry and smoky-eyed, lips voluptuous, skin the colour and consistency of cold chocolate milk. 'I am going to Chicago,' she said. 'My father did not pay the Gringos two thousand dollars so that I would die.' At the mention of Gringos the crowd cultivated a new-found energy, roaring in unison, kicking again at the sides of the trailer. 'We will get across the border alive. We will rock the trailer over. To the right, everybody. Only to the right. On the count of three.' When Faviola was born her father sat sulking in the corridor at the hospital, pulling at his stringy black hair. 'How can I take a girl out fishing?' he asked a nurse who was passing by. The nurse shrugged, perplexed. 'The same way you take a boy out fishing?' she asked, assuming it was some kind of riddle. Faviola's father thought about this for a minute and then smiled to himself before standing and re-entering the maternity ward. From the moment Faviola began to walk he took her out on the seiner everyday, teaching her to wrestle bonefish. 'Are we ready?' she yelled. 'One-'

José lifted his hand to his breast pocket, smoothing the outline of the chunky Nokia cell phone inside. His mother had presented it to him two days ago after one of her shifts at the bar. 'I didn't steal it,' she said. 'It was a straight swap, for a bottle of Tequila Sunrise.' José tried to believe her. He took the contraption out of his pocket and toyed with it, turning it over in his hands, lightly stroking the rubber buttons on the keypad. Any one of them would get him through to the American police: it was already pre-programmed to 911. If he pressed it they'd all get caught. But at least they'd be alive. 'Hola, estimos en untráiler. Nos asfixiamos.'

The dispatcher talked back to him in English. Nothing he understood.

'Nos asfixiamos. Por favor. Ayúdeme!'

'Sir!' the woman demanded. 'The address?'

'Estamos aqui. Estamos aqui-'

José realised the line had gone dead. He tried again,

pressing feverishly on all of the buttons time and time again, his fingers trembling with anticipation and rage. It was no use. There was a dim blue light from inside the machine that only served to mock him. By the time he'd given up many of the people around him were too tired to shout or kick out at the trailer. Every breath was like fire so that it hurt even to try. In the furthest, darkest corner an old lady was muttering the prayer for the dying. 'O Most Merciful Jesus, lover of souls, I beseech thee, by the agony of thy most Sacred Heart-' José struggled to hear the smothered words, making the sign of the cross. Like the old lady, he knew that some people were dead already. He could feel the souls lifting around him, the way he'd felt his grandmother's on her deathbed, a soft breeze on his skin as a flutter of invisible wings drifted above the bodies left on the ground. That day at the hospital, his own breathing had frozen momentarily as he'd watched but seen nothing. The nurse had felt it too, and rushed over to open the window. Now he closed his eyes and concentrated on the Technicolor movie playing on the backs of his eyelids; he and Lorenzo and his father out on the farm, hacking at the knee-length pineapple stems. He could see his mother's hands washing fruits at the faucet in the brick outhouse, and behind him, down the dirt track: the clumpy brown shoes of the village abortionist come to collect the pineapple roots that could sometimes accelerate his procedures. 'Faviola?' José's larynx squealed, seemingly of its own volition. He wanted to hold the mouthy girl's hand. 'Faviola? Where are you?'

*

Tyrone was approaching the second truck stop, south of Victoria, parking up in the empty rest area next to a vast tree-studded horse pasture. It was one in the morning; hot as ever. He looked at the girl. She seemed to be sleeping with her eyes open, the chocolate bar prized in her fingers, melted into the shape of her hand. 'Hey Brandy? You wanna zip in that store for me? The beaners need water. Say, thirty bottles, the stubby kind.' He put a twenty in her lap. She turned tortoise-slow to observe him, the tiredness of a child blinding her senses. 'Go on baby,' he said. 'I gotta piss.' He watched her cross the parking lot as he urinated against the wheel of the cab, her bare white legs iridescent in the reflectors. 'Everyone alright in there?' he asked, knocking on the doors of the trailer. He put his ear where the hole in the taillight used to be. There was a muffled sound, someone stirring.

'Sir!' a voice shrieking into his ear.

Tyrone jumped. 'What? Goddamn it.' He stepped up to the hole a second time. 'The door, por favor,' the voice said. 'Many people dead. Many people. Dead.'

'Dead?' Tyrone jumped onto the fender searching for the bolt at the top of the door, his hands trembling, a sickness developing quickly in his gut. As soon as he'd loosened the bolt the door burst open, throwing him to the ground. A long string of Mexican people charged out, stamping on him one after the other. Some of them slipped through the wire fence and into the horse pasture while Tyrone was still trying to get up on his grazed knees. He crawled back to the fender, the stony ground

155

hard on his fleshy wounds. He pulled himself up on his forearms. There were scores of bodies inside, hundreds; tangled together on the corrugated floor. He couldn't tell if they were dead or alive. 'Shit. Shit. Shit.' He limped to the cab, grabbing his cell phone from the seat. He called Abel while more and more Mexicans slid out of the back of the trailer, running past and around him, running in all directions, the phone ringing and ringing.

*

Brandy gasped at the image staring back at her from the blackened restroom mirror; her blonde hair lank with grease. She took a bunch of napkins out of the dispenser, mopping at her armpits. She bit at her lips and smiled at herself. 'Smile Brandy,' she said, mimicking her mother's voice. 'A gentleman'll never marry a girl who doesn't know how to smile.' In the store the clerk was busy with a magazine. 'Y'all carry water?' she asked him. He looked up, one eyebrow raised, gesturing at the fridge behind her. As she turned to open the door a Mexican man burst into the entrance of the store, shading his eyes from the light, his black hair matted with sweat. 'Agua,' he said, yawping like a toddler, pointing at the plastic bottle in the crook of Brandy's arm. He started towards her, his footsteps slow and clomping like a zombie out of a horror movie. 'Agua por favour.'

Brandy shaded her own eyes, squinting through the plate glass window. Tyrone had unhooked the trailer. He was climbing into the cab, a bandana tied around the lower half of his face. The freightliner started rolling. There wasn't enough time to run. She turned resignedly to the clerk. 'There're rattlesnakes in those fields out there, ain't there?' she asked him, the beginning of a tear stinging the rim of her left eye.

*

José woke up, a pain in his arm, sunlight shining through the mesquite foliage above him. 'Loren-' he said, the word trailing off. His head was pounding, his throat dry as paper.

'Loren?' somebody said.

José looked around.

There was a girl knelt beside him, some of a full, caramel-coloured breast exposed by a rip in her grubby white bra top. 'That your girlfriend?' she asked. She put a plastic bottle into his hand. It was very nearly empty, a few beads of clear liquid clinging to its sides. Still he sucked at it, more air than water. He noticed the pain in his arm was from a thorn, the skin around it pink and puffy. 'You've got a cell phone?' the girl asked him in Spanish. He glanced sideways at her, her thick hair tied into a messy plait, some of the strands loose and coiling. She prodded him, big hands like a man. 'You know the polisía came and went? We were hiding right here under this tree, watching the body bags coming out. I thought we were dead,' she held her fingertip to her throat and shifted it back and fore in a cutting motion. 'But they were called away to another incident a few miles back. They took the trailer with them. You remember?'

José tried to shake his head. It was too painful.

'So you call Loren?' she said. 'It's still dangerous for us.'

'You Faviola?' he said.

'Yessir!' Faviola said. 'Faviola González-Buendia.'

Punctuation

Beneath her the familiar sounds of Sunday morning had begun: her mother laying the breadboard down on the counter, her father arriving back after his walk with the dog, the door latch snapping in the hall. Silke remembered that she had woken briefly a few hours earlier, the damp bed sheet clinging to her as her body exuded a fever. She had dreamt of Lars and the way he'd bawled at her when she'd told him what she'd told him – a numb-skulled glossolalia, damp with saliva. She remembered him now beating the door panel with his fist until it split, his knuckles purpled.

'Silke!' Her sister was calling. 'Silke? Are you awake?'

Silke left the warmth of her bed and went in her nightdress to the guest bedroom next door. Ingrid was picking the baby out of the cot. 'Take him while I dress,' she said, passing him to Silke. Silke held the baby at his armpits, sniffing the fragrant scent of his scalp as she padded down the staircase. In the kitchen she handed him to her mother. The table was set with its usual assortment of condiments and cutlery. 'I'm so hungry today,' she said absently as she smeared a dollop of raspberry jam onto a hunk of caraway seed brötchen. She sat down, shifting in the seat, the wood hard against her pelvis. She was about to bite down when the lumbering silence of the room hit her like the butt of a gun. She looked up at her parents. They were gazing tensely at one another, the baby wriggling against her mother's grip. 'What?' said Silke.

'They've done it,' her father said. 'The barrier. They've done it.'

The bread was crushed between Silke's thumb and fingers. She dropped it onto a plate, rubbing her hands clean.

After coffee the sisters took a walk to Mitte to see the barrier for themselves, Ingrid pushing the pram. It was nine in the morning, the sun high in the sky. Already the air was warm and moist. Both women were wearing skirts, Ingrid's mustard-yellow. 'Did you buy that in the west?' Silke asked her, aware of the gravity of the question.

'Of course,' Ingrid snapped. She considered Silke's dress, quickly eyeing the sweetheart neckline. 'You?' Silke nodded. Friedrichshain Park was still empty, families of squirrels scrambling across the path in front of them. The sisters were quiet again; the only sound the whirr of the pram wheels. The further they travelled, the faster they walked; their mouths clamped shut, their minds turning over. Of course Khrushchev had threatened to turn West Berlin into a free city. Nobody believed him. East Berliners kept streaming to the cinemas and theatres in the west, buying subsidised tickets with their devalued East German marks. Silke caught the S-Bahn to the west everyday, walking the short distance from Lehrter station back into the east, and her job at Charité hospital. Nobody really knew where the east ended; where the west began.

As they headed out of the park and along the boulevard they heard the chanting, distant but frequent, carrying on a breeze. 'Schweine! Schweine! Schweine!' So, it was true. They did not look at each other. That would have confirmed it. Instead they kept walking until they came upon the Brandenburger Tor. A row of soldiers stood four feet apart, submachine guns strapped to their chests. Crews of workers in overalls were unrolling long reels of barbed wire and lifting them into the air, sharp, slate-grey stalks of bracken tangling over and around itself. Ingrid squeezed at the handlebar of the pram, her fingers turned white. Silke reached up, massaging her sister's sprung shoulders. 'It'll be alright, you know?' she said. 'You're married; they'll let you back in.'

Ingrid sniffed and lifted her head, forcing the tears back. 'What about Michael?' she said. Sweet, sweet Michael; Silke's fiancé. She'd met him in the first breaths of autumn 1960, eleven months earlier, late on a Friday night at the Café Einstein on Unter Den Linden. That evening she'd watched Carmen at the Komische Oper. The opera was a delicacy, her end of month treat to herself. She went alone. Lars hadn't the patience to sit for three hours watching anything. Afterwards she tended to sit at the back of the café and drink a single glass of red wine. On that night she ordered Trocken. 'I'll have the Trocken,' she said, and then, as the waiter turned on his heel, 'No, no, the Cabernet.' The waiter was used to her hesitancy and he stood waiting while Silke's choice switched back and forth like the pendulum of a metronome. 'OK, the Cabernet. No, the Trocken. Actually, what's the Tafelwein like? No, never mind. The Trocken. Yes, the Trocken.' The waiter bowed warily, concurring, and returned to the kitchen. The café was busy and it was half an hour before he brought the wine, by which time the large family on the adjacent table were stubbing out cigars and pooling loose change for a tip.

Their leaving revealed his face, puckish; grey eyes examining her from beneath a dark, curly fringe. His gaze rested on her for less than a second then moved onto an artwork above her head. She sipped at her wine, which was dry as a sheet of onionskin. She knew she should have chosen the Cabernet. Surreptitiously she used her tongue to wet her lips. The man's eyes met her again, and then moved, this time to the floor. Over the course of three or four minutes they continued with this mild, childlike flirtation, Silke concentrating on a specific feature at each glance: the thin veining of silver in his chaotic curls, the blueprint of crow's feet trailing from the corners of his eyes. Soon the game began to wane and she lifted her wine glass to her mouth, trying to drink, but already the glass was empty. She stamped the base of the glass on the crisp, white tablecloth; her lip sneered with disappointment. The man smiled generously at her and raised his hand to order more, the candlelight reflecting in his ivory teeth. 'Join you?' he said, approaching her.

'You're American,' she said, thinking aloud. 'But not a soldier?'

'A professor,' he said. 'At Humboldt. I hail from Ohio, the Midwest.'

Silke covered her mouth to giggle at his pronunciation of his home state. Oh-Hi-Oh, as if he was about to break into a canzonette. 'I'm a student at Humboldt,' she said flatly as she gained her composure, trying to draw attention to the difference in their ages. She was twenty-two, young enough. He was in his late thirties. But the point seemed lost on him. 'Really?' he slid her new wine glass towards her, nonplussed.

'No,' she said. 'I'm an orderly at the hospital.'

In the lull that followed she felt something between them, a kind of flutter against her skin, as if something invisible was brushing the insides of her arms with a feather. It was his eyes. In them she saw that he would care for her forever. Not love, not yet. Security. 'It's late,' she said. 'I have to go.'

'I'll walk with you.' In fact he walked two steps behind her, along Unter Den Linden and onto Prenzlauer. A deceptively light rain had begun to fall, licking their faces; his curls matting at either side of his head. Her blouse was sodden, grazing her cleavage. 'You may turn back now,' she said as they forked onto Danziger Strasse, her family home in sight. As he leant in to kiss her he smelled of rain and bergamot cologne. Lars worked at the zoo and brought the smell of it home with him – a warm, mown-grass scent, not unpleasant, but boyish and rustic.

Michael smelled like what he was: a clean, educated man. They saw each other once a week, concerts, theatre, excursions on the lakes. Three months later they were engaged, but Silke'd never recovered from the embarrassment of having tried to drink from that empty glass. Even now as she stood in front of the hour-old Berlin Wall, her mind's eye skirting over the memory of it, she felt the blush in her cheeks. Maybe if she had ordered the Cabernet after all, she would not have drunk the whole glass so quickly; he would not have ordered a second glass; she would not have broken Lars' heart. Every choice scrutinised, wrung of possibilities like a sodden kitchen rag. She could not let anything just roll off her back.

Ingrid was staring at her, waiting for an answer. Ingrid liked Michael. Everybody did. 'He's on a trip at the moment,' Silke said, 'with his students,' the words harsher than she meant them. It wasn't the answer Ingrid expected. It wasn't an answer at all. But she took it across the face, frowning at her sister's inability to commit to the severity of the predicament forced on them. Maybe she was too young. On their way back to the house they saw a notification from the GDR Interior Ministry posted at the entrance to the S-Bahn station explaining that easterners would, in the future, be issued with passes to visit the west. Ingrid consoled herself with it. She had to. She had to get back to her husband and apartment. She'd only come to visit for the weekend.

At the end of August, two weeks later, Silke was at work in the hospital. She couldn't take the train into the west anymore. She simply took a longer walk along

Invalidenstrasse. Everyone changed their routines accordingly, getting on with life without complaint. The barrier was treated as though it was an act of God, a punishment inflicted on them because of the Nazi crimes. Ingrid was still living at their parents' house. She filled her days writing letters to the GDR authorities. As Silke left the main building for the staff canteen, the rubber soles of her pumps squeaking on the new linoleum, the secretary on the reception desk called her back. 'A message for you,' she said, handing Silke the folded notepaper. It was Michael. He was here in the east. He'd crossed through the International border at Zimmerstrasse. He wanted to meet her for lunch.

For some reason the café he chose was on Am Tierpark, opposite the entrance to the zoological garden. He'd taken a table out front. Silke could see him from yards off, smoking a cigarette, the waiter pouring his Turkish coffee. 'Why here?' she said coming up behind him. His jaw fell into its customary rictus. He moved quickly to offer her chair but Silke was quicker, throwing herself into it. Her feet ached from all of the walking.

'Will you be warm enough?' he asked her, his eyes wide with taking her in, his presence so gentle it was as if she was sitting down to eat with an angel, a ghost. 'It's safer here,' he said, his voice as low as his nationality would allow it to go. 'There're Stasi informers all over the border areas and we need to work out how we're going to get you across and into the west.'

'Do we?' she asked him. The waiter arrived, pouring Silke's coffee. Michael was silent, sat like a spaniel at a rabbit farm, leaning forward, mouth open. 'Two ways,' he said when the waiter had placed their menus down and left. 'You could go through the green border, but that's risky. There're snipers on patrol there now I'd imagine. The other way, the best way, is to use my sister's American passport.' Silke was half-listening, her eyes focused on the gates of the zoo on the other side of the avenue. The primate house was at the back of the enclosure, out of sight. She imagined Lars, filling the chimpanzee's troughs with their dried food pellets, the sunlight catching the blond hairs on his stubby forearms. There were parts of him that she wanted still – his bumbling energy, the glimmer of cruelty in his eyes when he took the last fresh roll from the table. Michael would never do that.

'Silke?' Michael prompted her. She looked at him once, and then back at the yellow-leafed Linden trees lining the avenue. A brown paper bag was drifting around in the wind. It caught momentarily on a branch before ripping and unhooking itself, plummeting in a zigzag motion down onto the ground. It landed in the path of a car advancing along the road, perishing under its front tyre. She had to make a choice. 'The passport,' she said. 'If that's the best way.'

'Do you understand what I'm asking you?' he said. 'If our plan succeeds you might not ever see the east again. You might not see your parents again. If it fails they could kill us.'

'We're engaged to be married, aren't we? You can't live here. I'll come to you.' She let Michael think that she was choosing him, and she was, but also she was choosing comfort; clothes and cosmetics, trinkets she couldn't buy on this side of the wall.

It was another week before the passport arrived in the mail, and then they seemed to cross an axis, the world spinning at breakneck speed. Michael picked a day, a Thursday in mid-September. Silke had to get her hair dyed, blonde to match Michael's sister's passport photograph. As if to torture herself she booked an appointment at Udo's on Fritz-Lang-Strasse, where Lars' sister Ulla was an apprentice hairstylist. She was seventeen-years-old, plump: a female translation of her older brother. She was wearing her assistant's tunic, brushing thick curlicues of grey hair around on the floor. She sat Silke in the leather seat and draped a towel around her shoulders, smiling at her through the mirror. Silke wondered if she recognised her, and if she did, had she forgiven her for her betrayal of her brother, or was she simply trying to be professional? She smiled back at Ulla. 'It has to be golden blonde,' she said, blinking. 'Like honey, not too light.'

Ulla patted Silke's shoulder. 'I'm not qualified to use the dye,' she said. 'My colleague will do it. I'll be back to wash it out.' She returned to the front of the shop, taking up the sweeping brush, moving the grey spirals around on the parquet. Silke sat obediently in the chair while an older woman painted the gluey lilac paste onto her mousey hair; the faint whiffle of pop music from a radio in the back, blurred by static. Silke searched now and then through the mirror for Ulla, and the cow's lick on her left cranium, which was the cow's lick on Lars' left cranium. She'd hoped that the bleach would turn her into a new person; the kind who could cut her memories off, as if with a scissors. Today was the day. She was embarking on an adventure; she needed stamina, pluck. But in the mirror it was herself looking back; the same, reluctant Silke with a new hair colour. She gave a generous tip, not to the stylist but to Ulla. She took the girl's fleshy face in her hands and pecked her noisily on the mouth. 'For your brother,' she said, running out of the salon, a tsunami of adrenaline budding in her guts. The girl stared after her, eyes crossing with a happy confusion.

At four that afternoon Silke met Michael in the Presse Café near Friedrichstrasse Station. The room was clotted with cigarette smoke and after-work repartee. Michael sat on a high stool in the window, the newspaper obscuring his face. 'Your clothes?' he asked as she joined him. He had asked her to make sure that all of her clothes, even her underwear, came from the west in the event of a body search. Silke nodded. Michael looked tired as he stood up, the fluting at his eyes deeper than usual. 'A drink for the road?' he asked her. He meant a drink for the barrier, a drink for the checkpoint, perhaps the last drink of their lives.

'Vodka,' she said. 'No, gin. No, vodka. No, gin.' She brought a fingernail to her mouth, champing down on it. 'Vodka,' she said. Michael left for the bar before she could change her mind. He came back with two drinks. They gazed tentatively at one another while they took long sips. They stood now in the midst of the crowded café, the bases of their glasses almost colliding as they swallowed.

'The colour suits you,' he said, lying, once he'd drained his glass. Silke didn't reply.

'Are you ready?' he asked.

Friedrichstrasse was empty, the sun at its lowest point. 'Let's go through your English one more time,' he said, as they rounded a corner, their footsteps leaden, their knee bones turned to iron. 'My name is Andrea Shields,' she said. The pronunciation was perfect but the accent was wrong. They should have practised more. 'I live in Dayton, Ohio. I work at-'

'OK,' Michael said, stopping her. He was so nervous he could hardly breathe. Her talking was making it worse, his lungs aching for sustenance. Suddenly Silke realised that she still had some East German money on her. She should have given it all to Ulla. She tossed the notes into the grass of a vacant lot and then they walked on. A uniformed guard was posted next to the last building in East Berlin, his body casting a comically long shadow across the cobbles. He saw them approaching; it was too late to turn around. Silke opened her handbag to take out the passport. She was about to hand it to the guard when it jumped out of her hands, landing on the ground. The three of them dived down simultaneously to pick it up. When they'd straightened they were all smiling, the passport clamped in the guard's gloved hands. The guard studied the passport photograph and glanced at Silke. Silke spied around at the city behind her, hoping perhaps to encounter Lars and a last-minute reprieve. Of course the street was bare and dim. The guard swapped passports, looking from Michael's photograph to Michael and back to the photograph again. 'Auf Wiedersehen,' he said in a thick Thuringian accent, separating the passports with a flourish, the way a conductor indicates a cut-off.

The couple walked, as if through syrup, their route lined with tanks and the rolls of barbed wire Silke had seen the workmen erecting weeks earlier. As they crossed the border, Silke sidled closer to Michael, a little unsteady on her feet. She took his arm, smelling the fear emanating from underneath it, a sweat turned rank as fox urine. 'You were scared?' she asked him, her voice thin.

'Weren't you?'

'A little.' So this was how it felt, she thought, to accept one thing, and decry another, to make a decision. She was exhausted but triumphant. She had let the new barrier punctuate her life with its first full stop. To dispel the clouds of doubt competing for space in her brain, she concentrated on her most basic need. 'I'm hungry, you know,' she said.

Michael laughed his benign chuckle. Later he would try to convince Silke to arrange to see her parents and sister at the border by writing to them in advance. Many of the East German escapees would employ this procedure as a final sense of closure, but Silke would not hear of it. 'How could I look my sister in the eye? When I am here with you and she's over there, with child, alone?' The way Michael would hear it, the escapees would barely make their relatives' faces out anyway; bunches of stick figures waving at one another from a distance. Still, they insisted it had helped. 'Help?' Silke would say, her voice rattling with sarcasm. 'I don't want it. I've crossed a line. I will not step back.' For now, Michael assisted Silke onto the U-Bahn train heading for Wanasee, and his apartment on the edge of the student village. 'What do you want to eat?' he asked her as they sat down.

'Chops,' said Silke, resolute.

'Not dumplings?' They were her favourite. It was the least that he could do.

'Chops,' she said. 'Chops.'

Acknowledgements

Acknowledgements are due to *The Big Issue*, *New Welsh Review* and *Planet* Magazine in which some of these stories first appeared, with thanks to John Williams, Kathryn Gray and Jasmine Donahaye who initially commissioned and edited. I acknowledge the financial assistance of Literature Wales in making this collection possible. Thanks also to my agent Broo Doherty, David E Oprava for reading an early draft of *The Family Yang*, and everyone at Parthian. For encouragement, support and sheer brilliance along the way, special thanks again to John Williams, and to Kathryn Gray who is the editor of this collection. And of course, as always, thanks to Darran, for everything.

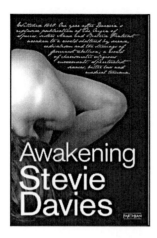

Awakening
Stevie Davies

Dream On
Dai Smith

PARTHIAN

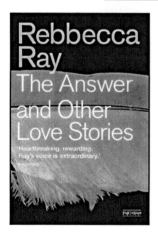

Rebbecca Ray
The Answer and Other Love Stories

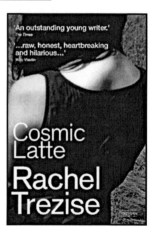

Cosmic Latte
Rachel Trezise

www.parthianbooks.com